Tricked

"Hey, Fred!" he called.

The man turned, scowling. "What?"

"It's me, Slocum. I run into you when I was passin' through Flag, remember?"

"Nope."

Of course he didn't. They'd never met, but Slocum had at least remembered where he'd seen the poster.

Slocum shrugged, pulling his Colt free at the same time. He kept his gun hand low so that Fred Whatshisname couldn't see it. "Must'a been someplace else, then. Sorry. I'll think of it sooner or later."

Fred turned to leave, muttering, "Yeah, you do that."

Slocum vaulted out of the stall and was behind him before he could make the doorway. "Don't move," Slocum growled when the man tried to turn around. "Hands clasped behind your neck. Now!"

JAKE LOGAN
SLOCUM'S
REWARD

JOVE BOOKS, NEW YORK

THE BERKLEY PUBLISHING GROUP
Published by the Penguin Group
Penguin Group (USA) Inc.
375 Hudson Street, New York, New York 10014, USA

Penguin Group (Canada), 90 Eglinton Avenue East, Suite 700, Toronto, Ontario M4P 2Y3, Canada
(a division of Pearson Penguin Canada Inc.)
Penguin Books Ltd., 80 Strand, London WC2R 0RL, England
Penguin Group Ireland, 25 St. Stephen's Green, Dublin 2, Ireland (a division of Penguin Books Ltd.)
Penguin Group (Australia), 250 Camberwell Road, Camberwell, Victoria 3124, Australia
(a division of Pearson Australia Group Pty. Ltd.)
Penguin Books India Pvt. Ltd., 11 Community Centre, Panchsheel Park, New Delhi—110 017, India
Penguin Group (NZ), 67 Apollo Drive, Rosedale, North Shore 0632, New Zealand
(a division of Pearson New Zealand Ltd.)
Penguin Books (South Africa) (Pty.) Ltd., 24 Sturdee Avenue, Rosebank, Johannesburg 2196,
South Africa

Penguin Books Ltd., Registered Offices: 80 Strand, London WC2R 0RL, England

This is a work of fiction. Names, characters, places, and incidents either are the product of the author's imagination or are used fictitiously, and any resemblance to actual persons, living or dead, business establishments, events, or locales is entirely coincidental.

SLOCUM'S REWARD

A Jove Book / published by arrangement with the author

PRINTING HISTORY
Jove edition / April 2011

ISBN: 978-0-515-14928-9

JOVE®
Jove Books are published by The Berkley Publishing Group,
a division of Penguin Group (USA) Inc.
375 Hudson Street, New York, New York 10014.
JOVE® is a registered trademark of Penguin Group (USA) Inc.
The "J" design is a trademark of Penguin Group (USA) Inc.

PRINTED IN THE UNITED STATES OF AMERICA

10 9 8 7 6 5 4 3 2 1

1

It was just coming spring when Slocum rode east, from California into the Arizona Territory. He hadn't robbed a bank in a coon's age, hadn't held up a stage in longer. He'd just been going from job to job, working on ranches and breaking horses, and lying low.

It was almost ten years since the end of the war, and he'd decided to quit fighting by stealing the Union blind. About time, too. Some sheriff back in California had recognized him, and had been dogging him for thirty-odd miles of hard country. About a week ago, he'd finally had to shoot him. Hadn't killed him, though. Just wounded him bad enough that he'd stop following.

Strangely, he felt kind of good about that part—the just wounding him part, that was. It made him feel sort of . . . upright. And he liked it.

His mount was his usual favorite—an Appaloosa. This one was black—shiny, glossy black, black as a raven's wing— with two white socks behind, a narrow blaze down the center of his face, and a blanket of snowy white over his rump. In the white patch were numerous spots, from the size of a big man's palm to dots the size of small pebbles. The stallion's name had been Rocky when he bought him, and Slocum had kept it.

Rocky had belonged to Slocum for three years now, and he'd never had a steadier mount. This was unusual for a stud horse. He was also a kind horse, if a horse can be said to be kind, and had saved Slocum's bacon on several occasions. This was a thing a man didn't easily forget, and Slocum hadn't. Rocky received only the best of care, and Slocum carried a pocket full of lemon drops—Rocky's sole weakness— at all times.

Well, Rocky had another weakness, too. Slocum guessed that he'd left behind about a half-dozen gravid mares in just the three years that Slocum had owned him. He chuckled to himself. Wasn't any skin off his nose, but he'd bet that there were a few cowhands that came up surprised when their mares foaled Appys.

Slocum and Rocky were heading loosely in the direction of Tucson. It was a town with not much going on, but it'd make a decent stopover on his way up to Phoenix. Course, there wasn't much going on up there either, but maybe there was some work to be found.

He was crossing the desert, west to east, had been for some time, he supposed. But he wasn't missing company. He liked traveling on his own, hated the way other folks seemed to keep on yammering at him just to fill the air with sound. But the air was all right with him, just as it was. And it was plenty noisy already. The scuttle of desert quail and the flurry of wings when he rode too close; the light, steady tread of a roadrunner on the hunt; the surprised slither and rattle of a snake . . .

He knew which to avoid, and so did Rocky. They were turning into quite a twosome.

There wasn't much country left between him and Tucson now, he realized. Just up around the tip of the Santa Ritas, then south a few miles. He wondered if the Presidio was still there, or if the town had grown over it the way it had grown most of the way over the swamp on its west end. There used to be a lot of malaria over there.

Rocky sensed his urgency, and moved into a slow jog trot. Slocum barely noticed. That was another thing about Rocky: he had the smoothest trot any man could ask for in a saddle mount.

He let Rocky jog on for a few miles, then slowed him back to a walk and started climbing. There was a little pass he knew of that would save them an hour or two of saddle time, and he was all for that. He knew that Rocky was, too.

By midafternoon, he had crossed through the Santa Ritas and was starting to follow the old riverbed that would lead him to Tucson, when he noticed that the birds had stopped singing. He reined in Rocky and sat there for a moment, scowling while he looked around. There was nothing that could have startled the wildlife into silence. Nothing he saw right away anyhow. But he did spot a covey of quail in the distance, a covey that had taken flight, and then he heard a rifle's blast.

One of the birds, a black speck in the distance, spiraled down.

It took the time for the bird to hit the ground before Slocum realized the shot had come from somewhere between himself and the birds. Scowling, he cursed himself under his breath. *You could'a been shot in that time, you jughead,* he thought, and reined Rocky forward. Despite what he'd been thinking, if the guy shooting birds up there had wanted to kill him, he'd be dead already.

He might as well go on in and be neighborly. Say howdy and all that.

He hadn't gone more than fifty feet ahead when he spied the shooter. Dressed in jeans, a blue shirt, and a leather vest, he was kneeling down, making a small fire. The quail he'd just shot was at his side, and a sorrel and white pinto was ground-tied back a ways, eating from a nosebag.

Slocum didn't recognize him, but he called, "Hello, the camp!" anyway.

The man looked up, saw him, and waved him in. *He's friendly anyhow,* Slocum thought as he rode toward the man and his scanty campsite. He rode up to the fledgling fire, reined in Rocky, and said, "Howdy."

"Howdy, your own self," the cowhand replied. "I'd ask you to stay and share, but I only shot me the one," he added apologetically, and indicated the quail on the ground.

"Don't fret over it," Slocum replied with a soft grin. "I was plannin' on makin' Tucson before dark anyhow. Havin' a hotel meal."

The cowhand's head tipped. "Is Tucson that close? Been ridin' down from Phoenix, and I ain't never been this way before."

Slocum nodded. "You can ride down with me, if you want. It's only about five miles or so."

The man, about six or eight years Slocum's junior, stood up and began to kick dirt over his little fire. "Sure, you bet! Didn't know I was so near to it. By the way, my name's Tandy. Jack Tandy." He stepped closer and stuck up his hand.

Slocum reached down, took it, and gave it a firm shake. "I'm Slocum. Just Slocum. What takes you to Tucson, Jack?"

Jack shrugged his shoulders. "Work, I guess. If I can find me some, that is. How 'bout you?"

Slocum leaned forward in the saddle and rested his palms on the saddle horn. "Same thing, I reckon. What kind'a work you lookin' for?"

"Whatever I can get," Jack replied as he saddled his mare.

"I'd like ranch work, but I'll take whatever comes along. I worked on a ranch up near Strawberry for a long time, did time workin' in a mercantile in Flag for a spell. Took a job of work down to Prescott for a little while, too, brandin' calves. In Phoenix, I done a bunch of stuff. Tended bar, waited tables, you name it."

Slocum smiled. "Jack of all trades, then."

Jack grinned. "Reckon so, reckon so." His horse was ready to go. He swept up the dead quail, tucked it in his saddlebag, then swung up on the pinto. "I'm ready if you are."

Slocum nodded. They set off for Tucson at a jog.

Jack Tandy proved to be an affable companion on the trail, Slocum decided. He didn't carp or rattle on about nothing, only asked questions when he really needed an answer, and seemed grateful to be riding alongside Slocum.

And surprisingly, Slocum was actually glad for the company.

They rode into Tucson just before dark, put their horses up at the livery, then moseyed on over to the nearest saloon, which also offered victuals. They both ordered beer with dinner. They didn't have much choice in the menu. It seemed this particular establishment served only one entrée a day, and today it was beef stew and biscuits.

Jack offered his quail to the waiter, figuring that they were more likely than he was to do something with it before it spoiled, and the waiter grinned. "Reckon we can slip it into the stew," he said. "Cook's always lookin' for filler meat." Which left Slocum wondering just what they were already getting in the beef stew.

He didn't have long to wait. Plates of the concoction were slid in front of them before he had time to take a long, thirsty draw on his beer, and after a bite of the stew, he was pretty certain there was nothing in it but beef, potatoes, and an assortment of vegetables. It was pretty damned good actually.

He had just begun to scout the bar area for attractive hookers—of which there didn't seem to be any—when Jack spoke up. "You been in this place before, Slocum?"

Slocum grunted. "Once, I think. 'Bout five years back." He didn't mention that the other time, five years past, he had shot and killed a fellow called Vance Granger in this very saloon. He tried to put it out of his mind, and shoveled another bite of stew into his mouth.

"They got rooms to rent?"

Slocum had to crack a smile. "Only by the hour, Jack, if you get my meaning."

Jack colored slightly, then said, "Oh, okay. Never mind. Don't believe I can afford that right now."

"Bein' broke's a bitch, ain't it?"

After they finished their meal, they each had another beer, then ambled up the street to a place where Slocum remembered a clean but cheap hotel. It was still there, and they checked in, taking rooms across the hall from one another.

Jack said he was almost too tired to breathe, and bade Slocum good night in the hall. And once Slocum got inside his own room, he discovered that he wasn't much more awake than Jack claimed to be. He fell asleep fully clothed, lying on the quilt-covered bed.

He woke to somebody banging on his door. Light streamed in through the window, telling him it was well past ten the next morning, and he stumbled to the door, muttering, "Hang on, hang on . . ."

He opened it to reveal Jack Tandy, with a gun in his hand and a very serious expression on his face.

Slocum made a face. "Whad'you think you're up to?"

"There's a bounty on your head, Slocum, and I aim to bring you in." The boy looked as serious as a heart attack, and Slocum figured it wouldn't be a good idea to test him. He figured fine, he'd just go along to the sheriff's office and let them explain it.

He said, "Lemme get my hat." He swooped it up and settled it on his head. "You're sure you wanna do this now, Jack?"

Jack nodded curtly. The gun in his hand shook a little, but he held his ground.

"C'mon," he said, and motioned Slocum toward the door to the hall.

2

Apparently, Jack had risen early and done a walking tour of the town, because he marched Slocum straight to the sheriff's office and through the open door. Bud MacGregor, Tucson's longtime lawman, was sitting behind the desk, and looked up when they walked in.

He recognized half the team right off. "Hey there, Slocum! Where you been keepin' yourself?" He stood up and stuck out his hand.

Slocum took it and gave it a firm shake. "All over the place, Bud. I see you finally got promoted to the big badge." Five years ago, Bud had only been one of the deputies.

"Yeah," Bud replied, "How 'bout that? Ol' Sheriff Richter finally retired, and nobody else wanted the job." He shrugged his shoulders and grinned. "Nice to write back home that you won in a landslide, though."

A gun barrel poked into Slocum's back, reminding him why he was here in the first place. "Seems we've got somethin' to clear up, Bud."

"What's that?"

"Feller behind me is Jack Tandy. Believe he's turnin' me in for the reward."

Bud's face screwed up. "What reward?"

Slocum found himself elbowed out of the way as Jack moved forward, so he slumped down in a chair. He wished they'd stopped at an outhouse. He had to piss like a racehorse.

"I'm Jack Tandy," the boy asserted, his gun still leveled at Slocum. "And I got paper on him." He fumbled in his pocket until he finally pulled out a folded piece of paper and handed it across the desk. "He's wanted for murder, and I want my thousand dollars now."

Bud had the paper unfolded by then, and looked up. "Where'd you find this?" he asked Jack.

"In a little mountain town up north, name'a Fern Gully. And why's that matter anyhow? I got him, he's here, and I want my money."

Sheriff Bud MacGregor sighed long and hard. "Well, you can put away that gun'a yours, buddy. Them papers was rescinded just about two days after they was sent out. Thought they'd all been throwed out long ago." He turned toward Slocum. "Sorry. Guess somebody didn't follow instructions too good."

"No problem. You still got an outhouse out back?" Slocum slid his chair back with an audible scrape, and stood up. "Gotta piss."

"Help yourself," said Bud.

"Plan to. And maybe, while I'm gone, you can explain to him what happened five years ago." Slocum walked out the back door, letting it slam behind him.

When he came back inside—feeling much relieved, but still angry—Jack was nowhere in sight, but Bud was sitting behind the desk, smiling.

Slocum said, "You take care of it?"

"You're free as the wind, Slocum. But I think that kid is a little annoyed. Should be. Like to get my hands on the sheriff up to Fern Gully."

"You and me both. How long ago did the kid leave?"

"Just a couple'a seconds."

"Okay," said Slocum as he put his hand on the front door. "Thanks, Bud."

Outside, he found Jack Tandy standing against a post, his head down.

"Jack?" he said softly.

Slowly, Jack looked up. "I'm powerful sorry, Slocum. I never would'a done it, but I'm so broke . . ."

Slocum, all the mad gone out of him, put his hand on the boy's shoulder. "It's all right, Jack. I might'a done the same if I was in your shoes."

When Jack looked away and sniffed, Slocum added, "C'mon. It's a little early, but let's go get us a beer."

Jack nodded, and he and Slocum set out for a saloon.

They didn't have far to go. Tucson wasn't much of a town, but it had more than its share of drinking, gambling, and whoring establishments. They went into the Painted Lady, and Slocum ordered them a couple of beers before they sat down at a table near the rear of the place, and the barkeep brought their drinks almost before they had time to settle into their chairs.

"So Bud told you the whole story?" Slocum asked after he'd had his first sip of beer.

"Yeah, I guess. Said as how you shot a feller—"

"Vance Granger," Slocum broke in.

"Yeah. In a saloon. Said he drew on you first, with lots'a witnesses. Said when he got round to checkin' his papers, turned out Granger was a wanted man anyhow, so they dropped the charges against you and paid you the bounty. A thousand dollars." Jack looked like he was going to cry.

Slocum gulped. "Shit!"

Jack looked up.

"Didn't remember till you said it, but that thousand is still in the bank! Hellfire and damnation, I'm rich! And so are you, long as you want to ride with me." Slocum had taken a liking to Jack, and felt sorry for him, too. A thousand dollars was a lot of money, and it would go a long way, even with two of them working at it.

Jack blinked, his beer mug lifted halfway to his lips. "What?"

"Said you've got half, as long as you wanna ride along. Sound fair to you?"

"More'n fair, considerin'." He still looked flummoxed. "Way more'n fair. Half expected you to take me out in an alley and shoot me." He tried to laugh, but it was weak and only shook the beer in his hand.

Slocum put on a smile he hoped was encouraging. "Thought about it. For about a half a minute. But don't worry about it. It wasn't serious thinkin'. If'n it was, you'd be dead already."

Jack sank back in his chair, and Slocum could tell the kid didn't figure he was kidding. He said, "Easy, boy. I'm just razzin' you. But I'm serious about the cash. You wanna think on it?"

Jack slumped forward and put his elbows on the table. "What you aimin' to do?"

Slocum shrugged. "Fixin' to hang around here for a while, then figure to ride on up to Phoenix. Better pickin's up there. What with you all of a sudden wantin' to go into the bounty huntin' business—and I'm thinkin' that ain't a bad idea at all—Phoenix'll have a better supply of everything, including wanted men."

Jack's expression had, during Slocum's short answer, gone from pleased to disappointed to amazed and shocked to simply surprised. He obviously thought that Slocum had lost his mind and appeared to be wondering who to turn him in to next.

Slocum laughed. "Don't worry. I ain't lost my mind. I generally do like to ride alone, but you're fair company. You don't talk much and you know your way around on the trail. I reckon we could ride together. And anybody gutsy enough to turn *me* in's brave enough to hunt true criminal types, I guess."

Jack seemed to consider it, staring for a moment at his beer mug, still untouched, before he looked up. "Okay. Fine by me. Fact is, I'd be pleased."

Slocum stuck his hand out. "Welcome aboard, Jack. Shake on it?"

Jack took his hand and shook. "Thanks, Slocum. I 'preciate it." Finally, he took a sip of his beer, then let out a long, hard sigh. "Guess I was more scared than I thought," he admitted. "I'm fine now, though."

"Don't let it prey on you. Happens to everybody."

Jack seemed to take some solace in that, and the two leisurely finished their beers before heading out to find some breakfast.

As it turned out, their first bounty came in just a day later. Slocum had gone down to the livery to check the horses and was busily brushing Rocky when a cowhand walked in, leading a sorrel gelding. Slocum nodded when the hand looked his way, and said, "How do?"

The hand muttered something—Slocum couldn't make it out—and led his mount on into a box stall. While the stranger was stripping his horse of tack, Slocum couldn't help thinking that he knew the man. From where, he couldn't figure out, but he knew him. Maybe not personally, but he'd seen his picture at least. In a newspaper? No, he was pretty sure that wasn't it. On a wanted poster?

Now, that was more like it! If only he could remember the man's name, and where he was wanted. And what he was wanted for! It was going to take a lot of studying if he wanted to turn this whim into a profession, he realized with some dismay.

The man had finished putting up his horse and was walking out of the barn before Slocum remembered. "Hey, Fred!" he called.

The man turned, scowling. "What?"

"It's me, Slocum. I run into you when I was passin' through Flag, remember?"

"Nope."

Of course he didn't. They'd never met, but Slocum had at least remembered where he'd seen the poster.

Slocum shrugged, pulling his Colt free at the same time. He kept his gun hand low, though, so that Fred Whatshisname couldn't see it. "Must'a been someplace else, then. Sorry. I'll think of it sooner or later."

Fred turned to leave, muttering, "Yeah, you do that." Slocum vaulted out of the stall and was behind him before he could make the doorway. "Don't move," Slocum growled when the man tried to turn around. "Hands clasped behind your neck. Now!"

When Fred grudgingly complied, Slocum poked him in the middle of his back with the Colt's nose. "We're gonna walk down to see the sheriff now." Quickly, he disarmed the man, relieving him of a rifle, two handguns, and a pocket gun.

Fred gave a deep sigh that made Slocum pretty certain he had the right man. Course, he figured that if he didn't, there'd just be a little embarrassment down at Bud's office, and a lot of apologizing to Fred. He could deal with both on the chance that it *was* the right man.

They neared the sheriff's office. "Right here," said Slocum.

Fred growled something nasty at him, but Slocum didn't catch it, and didn't care to ask him to repeat it. He just wanted to get the sonofabitch delivered as soon as possible. Quickly, he reached to open the door, then shoved Fred inside.

The office was empty. No Bud, not even a drunk sleeping it off.

Grunting "Goddammit" under his breath, he dumped Fred's artillery on the desk, grabbed the cell keys off their wall peg, and marched Fred to the first cell. After he unlocked it and put Fred inside, he turned the key again with a sense of satisfaction. That had felt actually . . . good!

Surprised at himself, Slocum found paper and pen and scratched out a note to the sheriff saying, "Bud, Happy Birthday. Brought you the man in the cell. Slocum." He put the note on the pile of guns and exited the office feeling proud and happy.

He just wished he could remember that fellow's last name!

When he met Jack for lunch, the kid clued him in. Seems he'd paid more attention than Slocum to the actual words on the posters lining the bulletin board behind Bud's desk.

"Daltry," he said right off. "Fred Daltry." And then his eyebrows shot up. "You took in Fred Daltry?"

Slocum nodded, then swallowed. "Guess so. What's he pay anyhow?"

"Fifteen hundred," Jack managed to say through slack jaws. "H-He killed a man down to Bisbee. And stuck up a couple of stage stops. And some other stuff. I forget."

Slocum nodded. "I suppose we'd best get back down to the sheriff's office and settle up with Bud, then."

Still wearing his napkin tucked around his neck, Jack shot to his feet.

Slocum waved him back down. "Get back to your biscuits. I meant after lunch."

3

The man Slocum had locked up turned out to be, indeed, Fred Daltry, and the paper on him was still good. Bud gave Jack and Slocum a voucher for fifteen hundred dollars, cashable at any bank in the Territory. Slocum was glad for the easy money, but Jack was beside himself with glee.

"And I get half?" he asked for the third time as they walked back from Bud's office.

And for the third time, Slocum answered him, "Yes, goddammit! Stop jumpin' around. Folks are starin'."

Jack muttered, "Sorry, sorry," but he couldn't keep from half skittering, half dancing along the boardwalk. "You sure about this? That you don't mind? Are you sure?" he asked again.

Slocum stopped walking and, with a sigh, pulled out his fixings pouch. By the time he'd finished rolling the quirlie, Jack had walked ahead a half block, realized Slocum wasn't there, looked around, then run back up the walk and skidded to a halt beside him.

Panting, he asked again, "You sure? I mean, you caught him alone!"

"We made a deal," Slocum said. "I'm stickin' to it."

"Well, we hadn't made the deal when you shot the first feller." He dug in his pockets. "I'm givin' you that part back, no arguments."

Slocum thought about it for a second. "All right. Reckon that's fair enough." He took the money, stuffing it in his pockets.

"I'll owe you seven bucks more outta the reward, okay?"

Slocum struck a match and employed it on his quirlie, then shook it out. "Don't worry about it," he said, setting off again with the younger man tagging at his heels.

"Where we goin'?"

"The bank, the tobacconist's for cigars, then a saloon, okay?"

"You mad?"

"No, but I'm gonna be if you don't shut up pretty damn soon."

After that, Jack only spoke when he was spoken to. For the day anyhow.

That evening, Slocum partook in the pleasures of a little blond whore he found down at the Oriental Saloon. Partook several times, that was. She was a pretty little thing, with round hips and full breasts and long legs that she curled up around his back as she bucked. At about two in the morning he let her run off, with a tip of about five dollars in her bloomers. They were both exhausted, and rightly so.

He woke at about nine, which was late for him, and busied himself rounding up his gear in preparation to leave. He had breakfast, then went to the general store to stock up for the trip. Even though it wouldn't be a long one, he didn't want to have to rely on game to see him through, and he doubted that Jack did either.

After a few more errands, he took himself down to the livery, where he deposited his parcels and brushed down Rocky. The horse was fit and rested. "And you're gonna stay that way, ol' son, with the bag of oats and corn I bought you," he murmured, running his hand down the horse's silky neck.

He took a gander at Jack's mare, too, and found her in troubling condition. She was coming into season, by the looks of her. Not a good thing when the only other horse on the trail would be his stallion. But he figured that she wouldn't be receptive to a stud for about a week or so. That'd give them plenty of time to get up to Phoenix, lock her in a stall, and wait it out.

He hoped.

He didn't know about Jack, but he didn't even want to think about what a pinto/Appaloosa might come out looking like.

He stowed his gear near the tack room, and set out in search of Jack.

It didn't take long to find him. He was out on the street, walking down from the sheriff's office, and he was studying some papers.

"What you lookin' at?" Slocum asked, once he got within shouting distance.

"Huh?" said Jack, and looked around until he spotted Slocum coming toward him. "Oh. Howdy!" When Slocum reached him, he held out the papers, saying, "Sheriff Bud gave me his extras. Figured to study on 'em on the way to Phoenix." He fanned out the stack, exposing a sheaf of wanted posters, both new and old.

"Bud says they're all up to date," he went on. "Says he

don't keep 'em if word comes down from Prescott that they're caught or pardoned. Or killed." He looked awfully proud of himself.

"Bud knows what he's doin', all right," Slocum replied with a curt nod, and then thanked Jack for having the presence of mind to stop by and get them.

"Don't mention it," said Jack with a self-satisfied smile. Although that smile didn't hang around very long when Slocum told him the plan was to leave today.

"Go on and get your gear," Slocum said. "I already checked us outta the hotel and bought chuck for the trail."

"Holy crap!" Jack thrust the stack of posters into Slocum's arms and set off for the hotel at a dead run.

That afternoon found them on the trail, well north of the point where Slocum had first come across Jack. They rode on a good piece, until Slocum sighted, in the fading light, the old ruin folks called Casa Grande. Slocum didn't know who had built it in the first place—Indians or Mexicans— but it was slowly melting back into the desert. It was reddish adobe, and two stories tall, although you couldn't get up to the second floor. That had fallen in long before Slocum had ever seen the place.

He pointed to it. "We'll camp in there tonight. If no pumas or Mex grizzlies or Apache have moved in, that is."

Jack looked at him, eyes wide, and sputtered, "Grizzlies?"

Slocum laughed. "That's the one what's got you worried? C'mon!" He showed Rocky his heels, and they galloped forward, toward the ancient building, with Jack bringing up the rear.

There were no animals present, aside from a scorpion that Slocum kicked out into the night, and the structure was vacant of Indians as well. This latter was much to Jack's relief—Slocum could see it on his face. It was a healthy fear, though. Slocum had spent a year or so living with the Apache, and he could personally attest to their reputation for being murderous thugs.

Jack being as jumpy as he was, though, he decided that now wasn't the best time to share the story.

Jack managed to scrape up enough kindling for a small fire before it got too dark to see, and started it going inside. He asked, "You get spuds, too?"

Slocum looked up from the stew he was concocting. He had set the beef on to brown up, and was just reaching for his vittles bag again. "Yes," he said. "And peas and carrots and onions and such. Now, you do your job and I'll do mine, okay?"

Jack flushed, muttered, "Okay," and got up to see to the horses, which they had brought inside with them. Slocum flicked an eye toward him every once in a while. He was doing a good job of it.

After Slocum had browned the beef, he added water and flour and salt and the vegetables, cut up into bite-sized pieces, and gave the whole thing a good stir before he settled the lid on it. Next, he hauled out the coffeepot and got that set on the fire, and only then did he lean back and light himself a smoke. It was a cigar, one of the ones he'd got back in Tucson, and it was damned fine.

About that time, Jack settled back in across the fire. "Done," he said as he reached into his pocket and pulled out his own fixings bag. He proceeded to roll himself a quirlie, saying, "Smells good!" while he pointed at the stew pot.

"Hope it lives up to the advertisin'," said Slocum.

Jack lit his quirlie at just about the time Slocum sat forward.

Jack started to say, "What—" but Slocum shushed him.

"Indians," he whispered, slowly rising, and bringing his rifle up with him.

He crept toward what had once been the ancient adobe's entrance and peered around it, squinting eyes accustomed to firelight out into the dark desert. It took him a few minutes, but his eyes adjusted and he thought he spotted movement in the brush.

He couldn't make out what it was, though, not yet.

He just hoped to hell it was something he could handle. Like a couple of coyotes out on the hunt.

He pulled back, spine pressing the adobe wall, and hissed, "Get your rifle and go stand by that window. Keep outta sight, but keep watch."

He didn't have to say anything more. Jack was up and moving across the adobe before he finished telling him what to do.

Once the boy was in position across the way, Slocum turned back toward the doorway, peeking carefully out into the night.

There was nothing. No sound of rustling brush, no shadows creeping from pillar to post, nothing. But Slocum knew the Apache better than that. Silence was their skill, and stealth was their forte.

And then he heard it: a soft, scratching sound at the back of the building. The sort of sound an Apache moccasin might make if it was unconsciously rubbed against the wall. He signaled Jack, pointing his attention upward.

And then, much to Jack's shock, he spoke loudly, in Apache, "Greetings, fellow travelers. I am Slocum, who was one with the people of Cochise for twelve moons. We have food, and enough to share. Come and join us at the fire!"

That said, he hoped to hell they weren't some other tribe. Most others hated the Apache, and any poor soul who was a friend to them.

He thought he heard a few hushed whispers, then a grumble and a grunt.

And then, a somewhat familiar voice spoke out, also in the Apache tongue. "Slocum! Is this truly you? It has been many years since our trails crossed."

"Come and sit beside our fire, Geronimo. I will add more beef to the pot."

"We come."

Slocum lowered his rifle and signaled Jack to do the same. In fact, he told him to put it under his blanket.

"Underneath? Why?"

"Do it, if you still wanna have it in the morning, okay?" Slocum growled softly while he quickly stashed his own in the same manner.

When the Apache began to come in a few moments later, Jack was as scared as he ever had been in all his born days.

There were only five of them altogether, but they looked fierce, like wild animals caged too long and too cruelly. And they were on foot. He wondered how long they had been without horses, and slid a glance toward his mare. She was still all right, but he saw one of the braves give her the once-over.

Slocum was still talking to one of the men. Now, he remembered that he'd heard the name before—when Slocum had said it just a minute ago—but he would have recognized it in any case. It was Spanish for Jerome, but more than that, Geronimo was a name to be feared no matter who or where you were.

And especially, he thought, when you were trapped in an ancient adobe wreck of a pueblo with only one other white man there to help you. And that white man was, as Jack sat there, patting Geronimo on the back and taking a swig of some Apache drink or other.

Slocum turned toward him and held it out. "Real tiswin, and it's mighty fine. Care for a swig?"

"N-No th-thanks," Jack stuttered.

Slocum laughed, said something in Apache, then all the men—not including Jack—laughed.

He supposed he was being made fun of. Well, fine. Let them make sport of him. *Just please, God,* he silently urged, *don't let them scalp me.*

4

The stew barely managed to go around, but Slocum supplemented it—with every damn thing he'd bought in Tucson for Jack and himself for the three-day trip, including half an apple pie.

He was especially annoyed to see that go.

But it appeared that the group hadn't eaten in some time. They shoveled in the food like they were starving, at any rate.

There was no talk during dinner. Right after, though, Geronimo thanked Slocum for the food—and said that the stew was too salty. Slocum just smiled, although he cursed on the inside. Damn stupid Apache! That stew had been perfect! Well, as perfect as he could make it, stretched out like that anyway.

Geronimo offered to stand guard through the night—to have one of his men stand guard, that was—and although Slocum objected, Geronimo won the argument. It didn't stop Slocum, though. He lay awake all through the night, keeping an eye on things, and didn't doze off until the Apache quietly pulled out, predawn.

"Bastards didn't even bother to say good-bye," he grumbled before he fell asleep.

When Jack woke up, the first thing he did was check for his rifle, and the second thing was to look for his horse. They were both right where he'd left them, and he let out a long sigh of relief. There was no sign of the Apache. But there was no sign of Slocum either. He propped himself up on an elbow so he could see out a window. Nothing.

"Hey, Slocum!" he yelled.

Right in the middle of the word "Slocum," there was a rifle shot—pretty close by, too—that had Jack up on his feet, rifle in hand, in a matter of seconds. He scurried across the ruin and peered out the doorway, his rifle up and ready, but he immediately relaxed. Slocum was walking toward him through the brush, a dead jackrabbit swinging from his hand.

Breakfast!

They rode throughout the day without further interruption from Indians, although Slocum noticed that Jack kept twisting his head like an owl, trying to scan all horizons at once. Slocum had to chuckle under his breath. He figured he ought to tell Jack that if he'd survived spending the night—and sharing a meal—with Geronimo, he wasn't likely to be attacked.

He wasn't likely to have a hair on his head so much as touched either. For one thing, Apache didn't scalp. And for another, sharing a meal with Geronimo was, to the Apache, something like having a sandwich with Jesus.

But he'd wait until tonight to tell him. He was having too much fun watching the boy's head twist back and forth, back and forth.

And each time they stopped to rest the horses and water

them, a sore-necked Jack was as jumpy as a jackrabbit, starting at every snap of a tortoise-crushed twig or flap of a sparrow's wing.

Slocum just kept watching and grinning.

They made good time, and camped for the night around thirty miles south of the Rio Salado, called by some the Salt River. Slocum figured they'd make it into Phoenix on the morrow. In the meantime, they dined on what little hardtack Slocum had saved back, and drank coffee. Cup after cup of it, just to fill out the hollows.

And when it was time to go to sleep, neither man could.

"I got the solution," said Slocum and dragged himself up out of his bedroll. He went to the horses, rummaged around in his saddlebags, and came back with a pint bottle of whiskey. He uncorked it. "Reckon we need to put this to some use," he said, took a swig, and handed the bottle to Jack.

Jack drank long and hard from the bottle, handed it back, then wiped his mouth with the back of his hand. "Good thinkin'," he said. "Thanks."

Slocum noted that half the bottle was gone. "No more for you, Jack Tandy. I ain't gonna spend tomorrow ridin' in circles with a drunk."

Jack nodded and settled back down in his blanket while Slocum took another pull on the pint bottle, then tucked it away. He pulled his last cigar from his pocket and lit it. The whiskey had worked. On Jack anyway. He was already nodding off. But Slocum had enough wakefulness left in him to go through half a cigar and carefully stub it out for later.

A man never could tell when a good cigar—or half of one anyhow—was going to come in handy.

When he awoke, Jack was still sound asleep, and the sun's morning rays—yellow, pink, and magenta—were just beginning to creep over the eastern horizon.

He lay there for a moment, allowing himself to drink in the beauty of it and wondering, not for the first time, why sunrises and sunsets in Arizona could be so glorious when the days were nothing but blistering hot.

At last, he got up, got the fire going again, and made coffee. He thought he could be excused. There was still a little nip in the air from the night before.

After he'd grained and watered the horses, he came back to the fire and gave Jack's boot a kick. The kid woke with a start and reached for his gun, only to find Slocum's booted foot stepping down on his wrist.

"Oh," he said, looking up sheepishly. "Guess I'm still jumpy from those Apaches."

"Those Apache," corrected Slocum. "No *s* to it."

"Oh," Jack said again. "Sorry."

"Don't 'pologize to me. Apologize to the Apache."

Jack was rubbing his wrist. "Don't believe I will, if it's the same to you."

"Might want to reconsider that." Slocum indicated off to the left.

"Oh, my God," muttered Jack. Five braves, mounted this time, were riding toward them. "Not again!"

Slocum raised his hand in greeting. "Hope they ain't lookin' for breakfast. We're fresh out."

"Maybe they're looking for scalps," whispered Jack.

"Apache don't take scalps." Slocum figured that maybe it was time to straighten the kid out. But it would have to wait. Geronimo himself came trotting up to the camp, followed at a respectable distance by the rest of his small party.

He spoke Spanish to Slocum this time, and after the requisite greetings were exchanged, Slocum admired his horse. "Nice gelding," he said in Spanish. "Good legs."

Geronimo nodded curtly. "He will do."

"Step on down, step on down. You boys care for a cup of coffee?"

"You have food?"

Slocum shook his head sadly. "No, sorry. 'Fraid we ate it all the other night." He expected the Indians to ride out, but instead, Geronimo dismounted.

As if he had signaled them permission, the other four dismounted, too. Geronimo said, "We will share with you, then." In Apache, he told the other braves to come in, and to bring their game with them.

And into the camp they came, bearing quail by the string, rabbits, and a couple of snakes. Slocum noticed Jack making a face when the Apache brought out the snakes—rattlers, both of them—but he shot him a look that said, *Shut up if you want to keep on livin'*, and Jack let his face go blank and his gaze drop.

A wise young man, Slocum thought.

With all the Apache plucking or skinning, then gutting the game, it was ready to cook in no time. Slocum brought out his skillets, Geronimo's men made spits to roast most of the quail, and the meat was done in no time. As they had the other night, the Indians drank only water with their meal, so Slocum and Jack had the whole pot of coffee to themselves. Jack even took himself a small piece of snake—just to appear sociable, Slocum thought—and managed to down it without gagging. He did a whole lot better with the quail and jackrabbit, Slocum noticed.

And all the while, Slocum watched Geronimo's horses. They were newly pilfered from some poor rancher, he figured. All the mounts were fat and healthy. It was his guess that Geronimo's boys had picked out the best to butcher, while they were at it. Just in case.

"You stare at our horses, Slocum," Geronimo said. "Why? Do you want to trade?"

Slocum shook his head. "Just wondering if you'd like some water for them."

"No. We have water. We will see to it later."

The horses looked parched to him, but he knew better than to argue with an Apache, especially this one. He just nodded and let it slide.

He was much relieved when Geronimo at last stood up—and all his men with him—and walked toward their horses. And even more relieved when they broke out their water and let their horses drink deep.

Afterward, they jumped on their mounts, waved good-bye, and took off toward the east.

Jack, who had remained silent throughout the visit, breathed, "Jesus God."

Slocum looked at the mess of bones the Apache had left, and said, "Yup." Ignoring the half cigar in his pocket, he rolled himself a quirlie, lit it with a twig from the fire, and settled back with his last cup of coffee.

"H-How can you be so c-calm?" stuttered Jack.

"Practice," said Slocum after a draw on his quirlie. "Just practice." He began clueing Jack in on Apache fundamentals.

"And so, you don't need to be so skittish, long as Geronimo's the one hauntin' this particular plain," Slocum said, by way of closing. He thought he'd remembered everything. "That's all there is to it. Feel better now?"

Jack, who had sat silently through the explanation, grudgingly said, "Some, I guess. But that don't change the fact that Apaches—I mean Apache—killed my uncle and his wife. They was good people. They didn't deserve it."

"Nobody deserves bein' killed," Slocum replied. He stared at the ground. "Especially by the Apache. But it happens, Jack." He lifted his gaze. "And you, you'd best start learnin'

Spanish. They all speak it. The other night, I think Geronimo slipped up 'cause I started it. Talkin' Apache, I mean. But generally, they think it dirties their tongue to talk it to an outsider. You followin'?"

"Yeah. I gotta learn Spanish."

"Good man." Slocum dumped out the last of his coffee, long gone cold, and hauled himself to his feet. "We're burnin' daylight. Best be goin'."

As Slocum gathered up his bedding and headed toward the horses, he heard Jack coming up behind him, dragging his feet. He supposed that Jack wasn't too happy about the visits from Apache, but there was nothing Slocum could do about it. Out here, you just had to deal with things as they happened. And you had no control over when and where they might take place.

Slocum decided to take one last piss, and as his urine spatted against a rock, he heard Jack behind him, relieving his bladder as well. Come to think of it, Jack hadn't got up to take a leak since Slocum woke him up! The guy must have a cast-iron bladder—that was all he could figure.

Slocum was finished, buttoned up, and on his horse long before Jack was finished pissing, though. That cast-iron bladder of his must've had pleats in it, like an accordion.

Slocum waited until Jack was finished and up on his horse before he said, "Ready?"

When Jack nodded, Slocum reined Rocky around and said, "Well, let's go!" At a lope, he set off north. Jack was right behind him.

5

Dusk was coming on when the two rode into Phoenix. The Territorial Capitol was up at Prescott—for the time being, at least—but Phoenix was getting along just fine. The U.S. Marshal's Office was up at Prescott, too, but that didn't mean that Phoenix wasn't a center of strength in law enforcement. The Territorial Capitol, in fact, moved back and forth between Phoenix and Prescott with disturbing frequency, causing some to call it "the Capitol on wheels."

Of course, none of this mattered much to Slocum. He still considered most of Arizona to be wild country. They had cavalry chasing Apache, Apache chasing cavalry and everybody else who happened to be in the way, rustlers robbing ranchers blind, wild mining towns still springing up all over the place and dying just as quickly, and everybody shooting each other with wild abandon.

In short, it was wild and it was woolly—just the way Slocum liked it.

When in a new town, it had become his policy to always

pick a good whorehouse and settle in there before he did anything else, and so he led Jack down whorehouse row—a street lined with grand Victorian houses and adobe casitas alike whose inhabitants all had two things in common: they were all female, and they were for sale.

He stopped in front of a big Victorian that was new—at least, it hadn't been there the last time he was in town— dismounted, and tied Rocky to the rail.

"What you doin'?" asked Jack, who had been silent for a very long time.

"I'm gonna to go get m'self laid," Slocum replied. "What'd you think?"

"Oh. Well, hell, I can afford it this time!" Jack was off his horse in two shakes, and headed for the front door in three.

The house was painted in full Victorian getup, with a pink body and the fancy bits done in red and green and white and purple. It looked like a four-star whorehouse to Slocum anyway. He smiled as he followed Jack, who was busy ringing the bell and trying to peer through the curtains on the door's window.

At right about the time that Slocum started up the steps, a comely young lady, dressed in nothing but pantaloons and a wrapper, opened the door. He heard her say, "Well, hello, handsome."

He heard Jack say, "Holy cow!"

He couldn't agree more. He came up behind Jack, and said, "You open for business?"

"Oh, you're handsome, too! This must be our lucky day." She stepped backward, swung the door in wide, and ushered them into a garish but well-appointed parlor. Several girls, all in various states of undress, lounged in the stuffed chairs and settees that ringed the walls, and on the ottoman at the room's center.

Again, Jack muttered, "Holy cow!" and clumsily—and belatedly—took off his hat.

Slocum grinned. To the gal who'd opened the door, he said, "This place new? Don't recall seein' it last time I was through town."

"Yessir," she replied, all doe-eyed. "We had our grand opening 'bout a year and a half back. Course, now we're under new management."

"New management?"

"Yessir, Miss Katie runs the place now. Mrs. Sloan went back East. She was before Miss Katie." The girl batted her eyes at Slocum, and beside her, Jack's posture stiffened.

"This Katie. She have a last name?"

"Sullivan, I think. Is it Katie Sullivan, Marcy?"

A blond girl on the ottoman sat forward. "Who's askin'?"

Slocum nodded, smiling. "Name's Slocum, miss. Like to know who I'm doin' business with, that's all."

"Might be Sullivan. Might be Dogturd. All I know's she pays me every week."

"Watch your mouth or it won't flap for much longer," said a new voice, which belonged to a buxom, leggy woman who was just coming up the hall from the back of the house. Redheaded and freckled, her blue eyes danced from girl to girl to girl as if she were tallying them up.

Maybe she was.

Slocum took a step toward her. "Miss Katie Sullivan, I assume?" He took her hand and kissed it. It was as pale and freckled as the rest of her, and she had the prettiest long fingers.

She tipped her head as she studied him. "I take it you're Mr. Slocum?"

"It's just Slocum, if you don't mind, miss."

"And it's just Katie, all right?"

"All right, Katie," Slocum replied with a smooth smile.

From the corner of his eye, he could see Jack watching him, open-mouthed. Slocum supposed he had the right. He'd said more to Katie in the last three minutes than he'd said all day on the trail. "I wonder . . . Would you do me the honor of goin' upstairs with me?"

Two of the girls slapped hands over their own mouths, and another dropped her cigarette on the floor.

"Don't mind if I do, Slocum," Katie said, smiling warmly, and put her arm through his. "Don't you burn my rug, Charlene."

Halfway up the stair, and blocked from the sight of the girls, Katie whispered, "Slocum, you old liar! How come you didn't want the gals to know we knew each other?"

"Omission, honey. Omission ain't tellin' a lie." They reached the landing, and he gave her a hug. "It's sure good to see you, Katie. Mighty fine."

"And you, too, you darlin' man." She stood on her tip-toes and kissed him long and hard on the lips.

"Mmmmm. You taste this good all over?"

"That's for you to find out, baby," she purred back.

He was about to speak again when they both heard boots coming up the stairs. It had to be Jack and his pick of the litter.

"In here," Katie whispered, and pulled him into one of the rooms. It had to be hers. She'd always loved knickknacks and little geegaws, and the place was full of them: on the tables, on the windowsills, and on the dresser tops.

Slocum leaned against the door and, behind his back, locked it.

She raised a brow. "Don't you want me to go anywhere?"

"Not for a month of Sundays, honey." He pulled her closer. "Not for a real long time."

* * *

It was coming near dawn, according to the cuckoo clock on the wall, and Slocum had worn Katie out. He'd worn himself down to a nub, too. What a woman! She had the most fabulous figure he'd ever seen, in or out of clothes, and that face? Her face was pure Ireland. Sometimes he half expected to find shamrocks tucked behind her ears. His folks were Irish, too—black Irish, they were called, on account of they were supposed to have some Spanish blood from back when the storms turned Spain's armada around and drove them onto the coasts of Ireland.

Katie lay slumbering on the bed, fully exposed to the warm Phoenix breeze coming through the window behind him. She'd come six times, by his count. Maybe more. It was harder to tell with some women than with others.

Leisurely, he rolled himself a quirlie and lit it, still staring at Katie. God, she was glorious. She'd told him that starting the moment Mrs. Sloan took off—after an uncle died and left her a big house back East, in Maryland—she hadn't turned so much as one trick. She told him she was waiting for him to come back.

That's what she told him anyway.

And he was in the mood to believe her.

She stirred, and he quickly whisked the smoke in the air with his hand. He didn't want it to wake her. But it had. She yawned, rubbed her eyes, then sat up. "What you doin' clear over there, sugar?"

"Thinkin' about you, little darlin'." He took another drag on his smoke.

She patted the sheets beside her. "Why don't you come over and think about me from here?"

He stubbed out his quirlie in a little cut crystal ashtray among the bric-a-brac. "Think I might just do that," he said, rising like a great cat uncurling from a state of repose. He strode to the bed, naked as a jaybird, and sat down. Katie was still sitting up, and he stuck his thumb and forefinger in his mouth, then applied them first to one nipple, then the other.

Both tightened up immediately into tight little buds.

Slocum's mouth quirked up into a grin. "Lawsey, Miss Katie, I do believe you need seein' to!"

"Oh, I do, Dr. Slocum, I do!" Her hands came up to hug her breasts even as she lay down. Her fingers worked at her nipples. "But could you try and fix it from the inside?"

He nodded gravely as he moved to cover her with his body. "Yes, Miss Katie, that always seems to give you some relief, doesn't it?" He nudged her legs farther apart, and she lifted them to hug his sides.

"Oh, Doc Slocum," she whispered, "I'm so grateful that you're here in my time of need . . ."

He plunged into her, sinking himself deep into her hot, wet core. She buried her face in his chest and moaned hungrily against him as he drove his shaft into her again and again. He couldn't believe how insatiable she was. He'd given her everything he had the night before, and she still wanted more. She cried out for it.

His hands found her breasts and squeezed and kneaded them as he continued to stroke himself in and out of her, gathering speed. He leaned down to lick and suck on her rock-hard and succulent nipples. Katie arched her back, pushing his tongue harder against the sweet nubs. Just when he thought he wouldn't be able to last much longer, he felt Katie's body tense and felt the spasm of pleasure ripple through her. Her moist insides clamped around him as she came, squeezing him and driving him to the brink of pleasure and beyond it.

They both slept in until after ten in the morning, and Slocum woke up groggy. Katie, on the other hand, woke with a spring in her step. While she helped Slocum find his clothing, she said, "Wonder how that friend'a yours is gettin' along . . ."

Slocum pulled on his britches, buttoned them, and sat down to do battle with his boots. "Fine, I reckon. Hope he's up already and seen to the horses. I plumb forgot, what with seein' you again." He shot her a sheepish smile.

"Well, I'm flattered beyond words! I made Slocum forget about his horse," she crowed. "That takes some doin'!"

"Damn right it does. Do me a favor? Peek out that front window and see if the horses are still there."

She did, pulling back the curtains. "Well, there are horses out there, but not the ones you rode in on."

Slocum shimmied his foot down into his last boot. "Good. Jack's on the job, then."

Katie grinned. "Feel like some breakfast? Seems to me you must'a worked up a powerful appetite."

"You ought'a know. You were right there, workin' it up with me."

Katie laughed. "That I was, that I was. And I ain't had such a high ol' time in a month of Sundays. Hell, a year of Sundays!"

"Best be careful, or you'll Sunday yourself back a couple'a centuries or so. And you'd best throw on some clothes while you're at it."

She threw a pillow at him.

"Now, I don't mind you bein' naked one little bit. Fact is, if I had my say, you'd be naked twenty-four hours every day. But there might be some folks down there that I wouldn't want seein' you that way." Shirtless, he sat on the edge of the bed, smiling while he stared at her. Oh, she was a peach, all right! He threw the pillow back into her arms.

"When you gonna grow up, Slocum?" she asked as she rummaged through her chiffarobe.

"Thought I did that some years back."

"Oh, you know what I mean. When you gonna stop holdin' up folks and robbin' stages and such, and settle down?" She held up a pale green dress. "You like this one?"

He nodded his approval. "I already officially vowed off stealin', you'll be happy to know. Got me a new job. Bounty hunter."

Her nimble fingers froze, mid-button. "Killin' people? You sayin' that instead of stealing people's money, you're gonna steal their lives?"

"Not to put too fine a point on it, I reckon so. I already decided that I'm only gonna go after murderers, iff'n that makes you feel any better."

"Not much, but we can talk about it later," she said, finishing up the buttons.

"Good," he said, rising while tucking in his shirttails. "Got some posters I'd like to show you."

6

Most of the house's inhabitants were gathered around the kitchen table when Slocum and Katie joined them. Jack had, indeed, stabled the horses just up the street a ways, at the Diamond-Bar Livery. Slocum knew it, and approved the choice. Jack seemed pleased—and also very relaxed. It must have been a while for him.

They all breakfasted on a spread of flapjacks, eggs, bacon, and coffee, with blueberry preserves aplenty to top off their flapjacks. When Slocum finally stopped eating, he was full as a tick. And it was only then that he remembered the posters.

He dug into his pocket and pulled them out.

"Whatcha got there?" Katie asked as he unfolded them.

"Want you and your gals to have a look at these. Tell me if any of 'em have been in here, or if they've seen 'em on the street." He laid the posters down, smoothing them with the flat of his hand, then spread them out. "See anybody familiar?"

"I do," said a pretty blonde from the corner. She was so

41

far from him that Slocum had a hard time believing that she could see.

"Which one?"

She moved toward the table and pointed at the third poster from the left. "Him," she said with finality. "He was in here 'bout a week ago. That wasn't his name, though," she said, still staring at the poster disdainfully.

"What was he using?"

"Steve. Steve Wallace." The name on the poster said "Wall Stevens," wanted for cattle rustling and murder.

Slocum said, "Well, he ain't got much imagination now, does he? Where'd he take off to?"

"A saloon. That's all I know. Prob'ly passed out under a table somewhere."

"Hey!" said a brunette, studying posters at the far end of the table. "This feller just come in! He's upstairs with Pansy right now!"

The paper she was staring at was for one Tom Mitchell, wanted for several murders, among other things. It also said DEAD OR ALIVE, as had the one for Wall Stevens.

"Man, it's our lucky day!" said Jack. "How you reckon to take him out?"

"Don't plan to 'take him out' at all," replied Slocum.

"But it says DEAD OR ALIVE!"

"Dead's the last resort, Jack. We'll take him alive if we can. All right?"

Jack nodded, albeit reluctantly.

Slocum turned back toward Katie. "He been in here before?"

Katie signaled to the brunette, who held up the poster. "Not to my knowing. Girls?"

None of them replied, except the brunette. "First timer, I reckon."

Slocum shook his head. "Got no way of guessin' when

he'll be finished up and head back downstairs, then."

"He's with Pansy, I told you," said the brunette. "She won't care a whit if you walk in on 'em."

"That's right," said a girl next to her. "Pansy used to work one'a them pony shows down to Mexico. She likes her an audience. She also likes 'em hung like ponies."

Giggles erupted from several of the girls.

"Hush," said Katie, and the room quieted. "There'll be no bringin' up of anybody's past while I'm runnin' this house, and y'all know that."

Several of the girls muttered, "Yes, ma'am."

"Can we go wait outside the door?" asked Slocum.

She nodded.

Slocum stood and Jack helped him collect the posters, which Slocum shoved back in his pocket. "Best stay back here for now. I mean that."

A little strawberry blonde in the corner said, "Oh, I do love me an authoritative man . . ."

Slocum ignored her and helped Katie to her feet. "Where're they holed up?"

"You can find it. Upstairs, second door on the right."

"As I face the front or the back'a the house?"

"Front." Katie didn't look one bit happy about her house and place of business being used as a spring trap for outlaws. She was probably afraid it'd cut down business.

Quietly, Slocum started for the stairs, with Jack bringing up the rear. They tiptoed to the second door on the right, and Slocum put his ear to the door.

Bedsprings squeaking. Grunts and groans. A muffled whimper of pleasure.

They were at it, all right. Slocum waved Jack back across the hall and signaled him to be ready. Slocum himself stepped alongside the wall until his shoulder was against the jamb where it would open.

He would wait. He wasn't so cold that he'd do the fellow out of a last chance to get some lovin'.

For five long minutes they stood there, and Jack was getting visibly more antsy by the moment. Several times, Slocum had to shoot him a dirty look or mouth "Stop it!" to get him to still the shuffling of his feet.

And then, finally, the bedsprings stopped squeaking. Slocum signaled to Jack to get ready. As if he had to—the boy was poised to vault across the hall with both guns drawn.

Slocum took a deep breath, then took a step back and kicked in the door.

The naked girl in the bed clutched the linens to her chin and shrieked. The naked man at the edge of the bed started at Slocum's unceremonious entrance, but his expression was that of a snarl—a snarling mountain lion, to be more precise.

Slocum said, "Tom Mitchell, I'm hereby makin' a citizen's arrest of your mangy carcass. Get dressed."

"And shake out them clothes before you put 'em on!" shouted Jack from right behind Slocum. How and when the boy had got there was beyond him.

"What he said," Slocum ordered. The girl was attempting to get out of the bed on its other side, and he added, "Miss, you'd best stay put till we get Tom here taken care of."

She shrank back into the bed.

Gruffly, Jack said, "Shake out them boots before you pull 'em on, Mitchell."

"Why don't you just come in here?" Slocum said to Jack. "Don't like people barkin' orders through me." He stepped to the side, and Jack, both guns drawn, cocked, and aimed square at Tom Mitchell's head, slipped into the room, and in front of him.

"How much is this one worth?" Jack asked.

"Don't recall. Three or four grand, I think."

Tom Mitchell looked up from his last boot and said, "You don't know squat. It's up to five now." He actually looked proud that the reward for his capture was so high.

Slocum figured him for an idiot. Was he trying for a record or something?

Again, he looked toward the girl on the bed. Pansy, that was her name. He said, "Pansy, you got a silk scarf I can borrow?"

She looked at him like he was loony, but she nodded at him, then toward the dresser. "Top drawer, left side," she said.

Saying, "Watch 'im," to Jack, he stepped toward the dresser and took out the scarf. It was just what he needed—long and narrow. "I'll get this back to you in about an hour, Pansy."

She nodded, and he began to twist the scarf up into a long, thin, makeshift rope. "Stand up, Mitchell. Hands behind your back."

"Can't you boys never come up with somethin' fresh to say?" Mitchell replied with a sneer. But he stood and crossed his hands behind his back like he'd done it a hundred times before.

But then, Slocum thought, maybe he had. Maybe he had a gang in town that'd just be itching to break him out of jail once he got inside. Or maybe he was double-jointed, and could slip the knots. Maybe he did this all the time!

Well, not this time. Slocum tied the last, hard knot after tossing an extra loop between Mitchell's hands and pulling that snug. He'd be hanged if Mitchell could get out of this one! He poked Mitchell in the back with his gun barrel. "Let's go."

"Y'don't need to get pushy 'bout it," Mitchell said, then hesitated. "Can I have my hat?"

It was across the room, and Pansy picked it off the bed stand and handed it to Slocum. "Thanks," he said, then stopped. That hat was a lot heavier than it should've been.

"Hang on a second," he said to Jack, whose body language was practically shouting at him to hurry up.

He turned the hat over and peered inside. Other than a sweat stain, nothing. But upon closer inspection—and peeling back the inner band—he struck the mother lode. It was packed with all sorts of little jimmies and picks and pries: the tools to open any cell door. Or any lock, for that matter.

Smiling, he said, "I think you can just wear this down to the sheriff's office, Tom," and plopped the hat down firmly on Mitchell's head.

Mitchell looked puzzled, but didn't say anything.

To Jack, he said, "Lead the way, Mr. Tandy!"

Jack eased a long sigh that wordlessly said *Finally!* Then he ushered Tom Mitchell out the door.

Slocum turned toward the bed. "Sorry for the intrusion, Miss Pansy, and thank you." He tipped his hat, then followed on along behind Jack and the prisoner.

He hoped Mitchell hadn't lied about the five grand. Oh, what he could do with half of that! And he could do twice as much with the whole of it.

"Cut it out!" he grumbled to himself. "You made him a promise, and now you're gonna keep it." Slocum had a feeling that his new partner was as honest as the day was long. But he'd also noted that two out of the last two—the only two—arrests they'd made, it had been Slocum doing all the work. Jack hadn't done anything but split the money on the first one, and all he'd done this time was hold his guns.

Knock it off, Slocum thought to himself. *You made a deal, now stick with it. He'll get better. He'd better!*

He followed Jack and Mitchell down the stairs.

None of the girls were anywhere in sight, so as Jack

opened the front door and ushered—well, shoved—Mitchell through it, he called, "All clear, ladies."

They walked him—as cocky as could be, the sonofabitch—down to the sheriff's office, where Slocum went through the door first, then held it for Mitchell and Jack.

"You the sheriff?" he asked.

The man behind the desk said, "Who wants to know?"

"I'm Slocum, and the feller with all the guns is Jack Tandy. The other one's Tom Mitchell." He dug in his pocket for the poster, but stopped halfway.

The sheriff was on his feet. He said, "So this is the slime who shot two'a my deputies. Wish you'd brought him in dead!" He moved toward the cell keys, then grabbed Mitchell's arm and began pushing him toward the cells.

Slocum snatched the hat off his head just in time.

"Hey!" shouted Mitchell.

"Shut your pie hole!" snapped the sheriff, and shoved him into the cell.

When Mitchell turned around, as ordered, and put his bound hands toward the cell's food slot, the sheriff looked at the pretty green and pink scarf tethering his hands and grimaced. "Just what the hell'd you boys tie 'im with?"

"Silk scarf," said Slocum. He pushed the sheriff out of the way and pulled a pick from Mitchell's hat, which he threw on the desk. Using the pick, he got at the knots, and finally released the scarf, undamaged.

As Slocum shook it out, the sheriff said, "Cloth? You tied him up with a cloth scarf? It's a miracle you made it a half block up the street!"

Slocum held the scarf up and gave it a quick tug between his hands. "Not cloth, silk. It's as strong as steel."

A quizzical expression replaced the sheriff's scowl. "Well, shit. Didn't know that."

"Most people don't," said Slocum, and went back to the desk, where he pulled out a chair and sat down, telling Jack, "You can put your guns away now." He heard them slide into their holsters.

The sheriff came back, returned the keys to their ring on the wall, and sat down. "Reward's sixty-two hundred. Voucher okay?"

7

Slocum took his voucher up to the bank and opened an account with it. Jack did the same, except that he took a hundred in cash. Traveling money. He said he didn't want to be beholden to Slocum anymore and, in addition, returned every penny that Slocum had so far spent on him.

Slocum hadn't been too eager to take the cash after he took in Daltry, back in Tucson, but half of $1,500 was nothing compared to half of $6,200! He figured that Jack had about four grand now. Hell, that was enough to retire on practically. Or at least buy a place.

He suggested this to Jack, but was met with derision. Jack wanted to keep on doing this forever!

All things considered, Slocum wasn't happy.

Jack was, though. He half skipped, half danced his way back to Katie's place, and you couldn't have scrubbed the grin off his face with a horse's curry comb. Slocum found himself hating Jack. But then, there was that promise. He'd given his word. God forbid that they should split up now, and Jack should take it upon himself to go it alone. Hell, he'd be dead inside a week!

They both took Mitchell's horse up to the livery, as Slocum had promised the sheriff he would, and while they were there, they checked on their own mounts as well. Slocum gave Rocky a couple of lemon drops, then ordered a turnout for him, and Jack did the same for his pinto, which got Slocum to wondering: if he shot himself in the foot, would Jack copy that, too?

Even though he knew that would really be pushing it, he somehow didn't want to take the chance.

When they got back to Katie's, almost all the girls were waiting, and they had a party ready for the conquering heroes! The duo were treated to the best champagne and cigars that money could buy, and Katie was in the kitchen, whipping up something special for lunch. Slocum didn't know what it was, but it smelled damn good!

Katie must've put the word out on Slocum, because the girls weren't fighting over him. They were practically brawling over Jack, though. He looked like you'd never be able to pry that shit-eating smile off his face. And every time he told the story of the capture, it grew more distorted and he played a bigger role in it. And with every telling, Slocum grew more disgusted.

Finally, he stood up with his cigar and a fresh glass of champagne, and made his way through the chattering girls to the kitchen hallway. That, at least, was something. He paused a second just to get used to the somewhat quieter atmosphere, then strode on back to the kitchen.

Katie was busy at the stove, turning sizzling pieces of chicken in a cast-iron skillet. Slocum crept up behind her, and between the shouts and coos coming from the parlor and the sound of the chicken frying, she didn't hear him.

He waited until she put her fork down before he grabbed her around the waist and asked, "What's for lunch, Little Miss Honey-lamb?"

It took her a second to realize it was Slocum, and when she did, she threw both arms around him, murmured, "You're safe, you're back," and laid a deep, deep kiss on him.

"Girl, you're makin' me want to haul you back upstairs again," he said with a grin. He meant it, too. Just the sound of her voice or the touch of her skin had him up and ready, and this time was no exception. And that kiss? Well, that had sure lit a fire under it, too.

But she shook her head. "Oh no you don't. It's gonna take me until at least dark until I can walk right again, you hound, you!" And then she giggled. "'Sides, I can't hardly cook on my back, now can I?"

He had to admit she had a point. And that chicken did smell mighty fine . . . Something else, too. "What're you makin' 'sides chicken?" He looked over her shoulder, trying to snoop.

She laughed again, then pushed him away. "You go wait with the others, out in the parlor. You'll see soon enough."

"When we eatin'?"

"Git now!" She shook her apron at him. "We'll eat when it's finished. Now, go on or I'll have to swat you!"

Playfully, he held his hands up. "Please don't swat me, Miss Katie! I'm goin', I'm goin'!"

He backed out of the kitchen, grinning the whole time, and set off for the parlor.

Katie was back at the stove, shaking her head and smiling and thinking that he was just a great big little kid when it came to food.

And she was right. He was.

He was the same when it came to sex, too—just an older

kid. An older kid who knew how to please a girl like nobody else, and who did it with gusto and tremendous enthusiasm.

She was still a tad unnerved that they had "arrested" one of her customers, and in her own house! It would have been different if Mitchell had been threatening one of her girls, but so far as she knew, he'd posed no threat to Pansy.

Of course, she hadn't seen Pansy since they hauled Mitchell away . . . Slocum would've said something if she was hurt or bleeding, wouldn't he? She snorted. Of course he would have.

She started turning the sizzling chicken again. Slocum was right. It did smell good! She peered inside the oven again and basted the roast, checked the biscuits, poked the baking potatoes, then returned to the stove top. There, she gave the green beans a stir, then the corn, with her big wooden spoon before she plopped into a chair and started fanning herself with a folded newspaper.

She hadn't lied to Slocum. He'd just plain worn her down to a nub!

Katie had, indeed, fixed a feast of a supper! As Slocum sat there, wolfing down roast venison and baked potatoes and fried chicken and so on, he couldn't help but shoot an occasional glance at Katie, and smile. Jack and all the ladies seemed to be having a good time, too, and Pansy—who had finally come downstairs—shoveled it in like she hadn't eaten in a month.

A couple of the girls picked at their food, sticking mostly to the vegetables, Slocum noticed, but all in all, it was a damn fine meal.

And for dessert, Katie brought out a cake, fresh from the bakery. It was chocolate with chocolate frosting, and she had one of those hand-cranked freezers full of strawberry ice cream to go along with it!

"If you gals always eat like this, I'm of half a mind to just move in, permanent-like!" he said around a mouthful of cake.

Katie laughed, as if she knew that would be the day! Several of the girls joined in.

Then Jack swallowed a mouthful of ice cream and added, "I'm with you on that one, Slocum."

More laughter followed.

Finally, they had eaten every last scrap of cake and ice cream, and pushed back from the table as one. Katie said, "Dishes, girls. Don't forget."

Mumbles of "Yes'm" came from the sated crowd, but it was clear that the girls just wanted to adjourn to the parlor for a bit and let that good meal settle.

And it appeared Katie knew it, because she sent them on their way with a wave of her hand. They took Jack with them, which left Slocum alone with Katie at the pillaged table.

He dug into his pocket and pulled out his fixings bag. "You mind?" he asked her.

"Have I ever?"

He smiled at her, then commenced to roll himself a quirlie. He struck a lucifer, then lit it. As he shook out his flame, he took a drag on his smoke, then said, "I mean it, Katie. You outdone yourself."

"Anything for you, Slocum," she replied. "I'll even cook that lousy pronghorn for you, just 'cause it makes you happy."

Chuckling, he shook his head. "Never did understand why you got such a distaste for it, Katie. You sure cook it up good, for somebody who's never et it."

She sniffed. "Too gamey for my taste, I guess. How much longer you boys gonna be stayin' on, now that you got Tom Mitchell?"

"Hard tellin'," he said, shrugging. "I want to make a

sweep of the town before we head out anywhere. If it's all right with you, that is. Don't wanna be a couple of burdens."

Katie put her hand on his arm. "You're never a burden, Slocum. Never."

At that moment, she looked particularly kissable, and he did—just a brush of the lips, just a promise of what was to come later in the night. Not that he wasn't ready, willing, and able to take her right there, on the kitchen table. But she'd said she was worn out, and Slocum respected that. He could wait, even though his britches were feeling awfully tight right at the moment.

He sat back and took another drag on his quirlie to help take his mind off Katie. It didn't work.

He tried conversation. "I thought Jack and I'd start hittin' the bars. Somebody's bound to have seen Stevens at one of 'em."

Katie nodded. "Just don't go gettin' yourselves killed. Promise you'll be careful?"

"Yes'm," Slocum said, echoing the girls. He smiled. "I'll try to avoid it at all costs."

"Worked so far."

"Yup, it has. And I'm countin' on it to keep on workin' for me."

He found he was finally able to stand up without embarrassing himself, and excused himself to go use the outhouse.

"Wait," Katie said, and handed him a lantern. "It's dark out there. Finn Macy just cleared out the black widows, and there's a Sears catalog for readin' and for . . . you know."

Slocum gave her a grin. "Thanks, darlin'."

"Oh, anytime." She grinned back.

8

At seven in the evening, Wall Stevens was tucked away in a cantina's back booth, in the Mexican part of town. He'd learned long ago that the quickest and easiest way to fool the law—to play around right under its nose—was to stay to the bigger towns, but stay in the Mexican or Chinese district of the city. Phoenix having no Chinese district, he'd been camped out at the corner of Third and Saltillo Streets for the past week or so. He was a booze hound, and he'd gone to doggy heaven at the Cantina Blanca.

Despite the fact that he spoke no Spanish—except *cerveza* for beer and *una mas* for one more—he managed. Most of the Mexicans spoke English just as well as he did, and most of them cut him a wide berth. He didn't know whether they respected him because he was white, or because he wore two six-guns and looked like he'd be ready and willing to use them at the drop of a hat. He didn't know, and he didn't care.

What he did care about was that they kept the whiskey

coming—and plenty of it—and that there were lots of hookers available. To both requests, the answer here was *"Sí, señor."*

He'd been staying here almost since he rode into town. He'd stopped at a decent whorehouse first thing, got him a pretty girl, screwed her like she wouldn't forget it, then came on down here, to the Mexican part of town. If the sheriff got to asking questions and learned he'd been at a fancy whorehouse a week ago, he was bound to figure Wall Stevens was long gone by now.

And Wall Stevens *was* long gone. At least, he was drunk out of his mind, which was just the way he liked it. He couldn't walk straight or talk straight, but he knew he had a room upstairs someplace, and that the pert little señorita beside him—who was smart enough to speak only when spoken to—would lead him upstairs when it was time.

And it was just about time. Another drink should do it. He signaled the bartender.

By the time that Wall Stevens had finished his last drink and stumbled up the stairs to bed, Slocum and Jack had already made the rounds of almost every saloon in town, and come up short. They'd found a couple of barkeeps that recognized his picture on the poster, but reported seeing him a week or so ago. One barkeep only remembered him because he was found passed out under one of the tables at closing, and they'd had to drag him outside to let him sleep it off.

The barkeep hadn't seen him since.

A dejected Slocum, who was anxious to get back to Katie, turned to Jack and said, "That'll do 'er for tonight. There's other places to check tomorrow."

Jack lifted a brow. "There are? Where?"

"The Mex places at the edge of town. That's probably where we should'a started lookin'."

Jack shrugged. "'Fyou say so." He caught up the two steps between Slocum and himself and began walking beside him, stride for stride.

This grated on Slocum for some reason. It seemed like the kid was trying to copycat him, right down to the last detail. He'd heard that mimicry was the best sort of flattery, but it had grown past annoying in this case. It had started back in Tucson, but he had just now realized why the kid was pissing him off.

And he really ought to stop thinking of him as "the kid." After all, Jack wasn't a decade younger than himself. Just young enough to keep himself out of the war.

He wondered if maybe that was it—the reason he kept thinking of Jack as "the kid." Even one little Civil War skirmish could pile a heap of years on a man. Inside anyway. Sometimes on the outside, too. He'd known more than one man whose hair had been turned white during battle. It was a miracle that his hadn't.

Of course, he was hardly ever *in* a battle. Most times, he was high up in a tree, rifle in hand, watching for officers. The Company sniper, that was him.

He shook his head, trying to shake the thoughts of war out of it. God forbid that he should get to thinking on it and start having those nightmares again. They were always ugly and pointless, and bad enough when he was out on the trail by himself. He sure didn't want to scare Katie with one of them.

So he said, "What you gonna do with your money, Jack?"

Surprised that Slocum had spoken to him, he sputtered for a moment before he said, "Keep most of it in the bank, I reckon. Save up, y'know?"

Slocum nodded, but then he pursed his lips. "Well . . . I don't know. Savin's fine and everything, but I figured a smart feller like you'd want to invest in something."

Jack's face screwed up. "Invest? Like, in gold shares?"

"Nah, that's real iffy. I was thinkin' more like land. It's cheap right now, but they ain't makin' any more of it."

"True," replied Jack, nodding. "True. Hey, how 'bout you, too? We could get us a ranch and be partners forever!"

Slocum had to consciously clamp his jaw shut to avoid answering that one, because "forever" would turn out to be about a week and a half if Jack kept on copying everything he did. Finally, he said, in a measured tone, "Nah, don't think that'd work for me. Got itchy feet."

Slocum waited for it. Finally, Jack grunted and said, "Yeah, me, too."

It was a lucky thing for the kid that they were well within sight of Katie's place, because it was only that which kept Slocum from simply pounding him into the ground.

They walked on in silence: Slocum, with hands at his sides and clenched into fists, which gradually relaxed as they moved through the white picket gate at Katie's and began to climb the porch steps.

Katie was waiting.

"Well, there you are! Took you boys longer than you thought, didn't it?" was the first thing out of Katie's mouth when she saw Slocum, which was after he'd fought his way through the throng of giggling women in the front parlor, and made his way back to the kitchen.

Katie was just drying her hands after finishing washing and drying what looked like a passel of plates and cups, glasses and serving dishes, and cookware. She smiled at him.

He gave his head a shake. "Can't you hire somebody

else to do that for you?" He took the dishcloth from her hands and set it aside, then kissed her. "You're too good to do the cleanup work around here," he whispered in her ear. Her beautiful red hair smelled fresh, as if she'd just washed it.

"Tell that to the banker," she answered with a grin. "Whoever said that a woman's work is never done, well, he didn't know the half of it!"

Slocum chuckled at her. She could sure live up to that red hair of hers at just the right moments! Still, he wished she didn't have to do it. Still hugging her to him, he asked, "Well, can't the gals take turns or somethin'?"

She stepped out of his grasp and cocked her tiny fists on her hips. "Slocum, baby, it's past eleven. Why don't you just shut the hell up and take me upstairs?"

One thing about Katie—she sure knew how to flip the subject sideways. In a heartbeat, he had his arm around her and they were headed up the hall for the front stairs.

When they got to her room and were nestled in her bed, she put her hand on his cheek and softly said, "I got rested up real good, baby. All except for my feet."

Slocum smiled. "I'll see that you're off 'em for a spell." He was hard as a rock, but waited for her to give the go-ahead.

She said, "That's mighty kind'a you, Slocum, mighty kind." And then she let her hand travel, beneath the sheets, down to his crotch. "Holy Christ! I'd say you'd best get to work on relievin' that swelling, and as soon's possible!"

She began to stroke him up and down the long length of his shaft. It was hard beneath her touch and growing harder by the second. She rubbed him gently and then began to increase the pressure, responding to the soft moans coming from Slocum. She wrapped the fingers of one hand as far around his thick length as she could get them. His flesh throbbed with pleasure under her soft touch. Then she slowly peeled back the sheets, knelt over him, and wrapped her soft lips around the head of his hard cock. Her hand tightened on the shaft below while she took as much of him into her mouth as she could fit. She had engulfed him so deeply Slocum could barely contain himself as she began to suck gently on his tender organ. She swirled her tongue around the tip of his erect member, making Slocum throb with desire. He couldn't stand it a second longer.

He grabbed her firmly by the waist and flung her to the side in one quick motion so fluid she barely knew what was happening. Before her remark of surprise had even fully left her mouth, Slocum was on top of her.

"Now let's see what we can do about you there, darlin'."

Slocum inched himself down Katie's body, licking and kissing as he went. He kissed and stroked her nipples, and when his hand reached down to explore her inner depths he discovered that she was wet and waiting. He lowered his lips to her moist mound and licked and sucked for all he was worth. Katie writhed underneath him, moaning and shivering. She lifted her hips to meet his questing tongue, driving him deeper into her.

He knew Katie was close, and he flipped her over once again so that she was straddling him. She smiled mischievously at him as she took a firm grip of his cock and guided it into her sopping wet opening. She eased herself down to take all of him inside of her and then began to move in short rhythmic bursts, up and down. She rocked her hips back and forth, stroking herself up and down his length. Slocum took advantage of his position and reached up to cup her firm and ample breasts. He caressed her hard, pink nipples and rubbed his hands all over her body as she rode him toward her peak.

Katie spasmed around him, and they came together, Slocum shooting his juices deep inside of her, flooding her already hot, pulsating core

She collapsed on top of him with a sigh of satisfaction, and they both slipped into a deep and sated sleep.

Slocum woke with a start some time later. He couldn't see the clock, but outside, it was still dark as the inside of a black hog. Careful not to disturb Katie, he felt his way across the room, snagged his vest along the way, and sat down in the stuffed chair beside the table full of Katie's knickknacks. In the dark, he rolled himself a quirlie and lit it, finding an ashtray before he shook out his match.

He heard a rustle across the room and then saw someone light a sulphur tip. It was Katie, of course. She lit the lantern on her side of the bed, then turned it up. "What's happenin'?" she muttered groggily. "Slocum? Why're you up?"

"It's all right, baby," he said softly. "Go back to sleep."

"Not until you come back to bed."

Slocum shook his head. As he stubbed out his smoke, he grinned and said, "Anybody ever call you a bossy little tart?"

"Not until now," she said, and motioned him to hurry up. "And I'd appreciate it if you kept that to yourself. Don't wanna be handin' out free ammunition to the girls."

"Yes'm," he said sheepishly as he joined her in the bed.

9

When Wall Stevens rose, his little Mexican whore was long gone. He shrugged. Maybe she hadn't liked his way of showing affection, or what passed for it in his mind anyway. He didn't know it, but she had fled the little bar with a bruised eye, a bloody nose, and cradling a broken arm, vowing never to go with an Anglo again.

Stevens didn't care what had or hadn't happened. That was last night, and ancient history. Right now, all he wanted in the world was to get downstairs and get himself some breakfast and some beer. No whiskey, no sir. It was only eight thirty in the morning, if the clock was to be believed.

He wandered down the stairs and emerged in the bar, where he sat at his customary rear table and ordered his customary breakfast: chili, toasted bread, and a beer.

This was the life, he thought to himself as he wet his whistle before tackling any food. Not like traveling time, or working time. Traveling time, he was either on his way to or his way back from a job of work. And his working time, he had lately devoted to killing people. He didn't know exactly how he'd fallen into the line of slinging his gun for cash—must have been while he was drunk or something, he thought—but it was surely paying off in a big way. He'd been busy lately, but the next thing he needed to do was to go up around Strawberry and kill somebody named Beau Martin, and he didn't have to do it for another month. So here he sat in Phoenix, living the good life.

Well, the semigood life, he supposed. It wasn't like Phoenix had an icehouse or anything. He really would've liked his beer cold. But he was used to it warm. It'd do. But it was almost gone.

"*Cerveza. Una mas,*" he said to the bartender. Then he turned to his breakfast.

Slocum was up and ready to go by ten o'clock, but it took until eleven for him to get Jack rousted out and ready to go. Well, almost ready to go anyway. Jack was still yawning and rubbing the sleep from his eyes as they walked the block to the livery and tacked up their horses. It wasn't that long of a walk to Mex Town, only a mile or so, but going both ways and all the walking in between was tough on feet that were accustomed to riding.

Once they got the horses ready and set off, they got there in no time. The town changed distinctly, from frame and brick buildings to small adobe, mud brick houses and businesses. The faces changed, too, from mostly Anglo to the darker skin of Mexicans. Slocum reined Rocky over to one side, stepped down, and tied him to a rail.

Jack followed suit. Of course.

They walked into a cantina called the Blue Heron—in Spanish anyway. It was typical. Small, one story, and filled with scarred tables and chairs, and a long bar. There weren't many patrons. Slocum looked around, and saw no white faces. But he decided to give it a try.

He walked up to the bar, Jack at his heels, and waited. When the bartender got down to him, Slocum said in Spanish, "This fellow come in lately?" He unfolded the poster of Wall Stevens and laid it out flat on the bar.

The barkeep picked it up and stared at it. He shook his head. In perfect English, he said, "No, sir. No whites in maybe two years. You would like a beer? Maybe whiskey?"

Slocum and Jack both shook their heads. "Not today, thanks," Jack offered.

The bartender turned to walk away, then suddenly stopped. He muttered, "Maria!" and turned back, calling, "Wait!"

Slocum and Jack turned back. "You remember something?" Slocum asked.

"I have not seen this man, but I know this reads 'dead or alive.' You must talk to Maria. Last night, she was . . . courted . . . by an Anglo. He broke her arm and blackened her eye."

Slocum nodded. He understood. "Where can I find her?"

"Two blocks south, on Ramona Street. The little casa with the red door and the green shutters. Oh, and her name is Maria Lopez."

Slocum dug into his pocket and pulled out a gold eagle, which he placed on the bar. "Thanks, *compadre*. I appreciate it."

While the barkeep studied the ten-dollar piece—and bit it, for good measure—Slocum and Jack slipped out the front doors.

As they remounted their horses and reined away from the rail, Jack, excited as usual, said, "What a stroke of luck! I can't believe we're gonna get him this easy!"

Slocum didn't share his enthusiasm. "Don't go throwin'

a party yet. Might not be Stevens. Even if it is, he might'a rode out this mornin'. Or last night. He could be halfway to Yuma by now."

All Jack said was, "Oh," and closed his mouth.

But when they came to Ramona Street, he got antsy again. "Which way now? Right or left?"

"Calm the hell down," Slocum muttered. "He didn't say, so we're gonna look. All right?"

"Fine."

Jack looked as if the bartender should have left them a trail of breadcrumbs or something. Slocum shook his head and reined Rocky to the left. They rode down about a block and a half to where the street ended. There was nothing beyond but a goat pen and somebody's truck garden.

They turned around and headed back to the crossroads, then down the unsearched portion of Ramona Street.

"This is more like it," Slocum said. It looked to him like the red light district he was expecting. All the little yards were well cared for, and the slouching adobes were brightly adorned, with colored fences, doors, and shutters.

"There!" Jack suddenly shouted. He was pointing to a white-fenced adobe, with a red door and teal green shutters.

"I believe you're right," Slocum replied. They dismounted and tied their horses to the rail. "Careful," he added, putting a hand on Jack's shoulder. "He might be in there."

Jack nodded, and they went through the gate and up to the front door, which bore a small sign. PLEASE KNOCK, it said in Spanish.

Slocum raised his knuckles and knocked.

After a moment, the door was opened inward by a middle-aged Mexican woman, her jet-black hair in a plait that trailed over her shoulder and traveled nearly to her waist.

"Sí?" she said suspiciously. Slocum took it that Anglos weren't common in this part of town.

In Spanish, he began, "Does Maria Lopez live here? We were told that—"

"Why do you want do know?" came the curt reply. "Did one of you break her arm?"

Slocum said, "No, ma'am. We're out after the feller what did it. If he is who we think he is, she was lucky that her arm was the only thing he broke."

"And who do you think he is?"

Slocum pulled out the poster again, and she studied it. She pointed at the name under WANTED: DEAD OR ALIVE. "This is not the name," she said.

Slocum turned the poster around and found the part with the aliases. He asked, "One of these, then?" He turned the paper back to face her, pointing at the pertinent paragraph.

She looked and looked and looked, and at last, her scowl curled up into a satisfied grin. "It is him. This Steve Wallace. I cannot say for the picture, though. I did not see him."

"Can Maria check for us?"

She thought this over while, beside him, Jack shifted from foot to foot. Either he had to piss awful bad, or he was going crazy from not knowing what was going on. Knowing Jack, Slocum guessed the latter.

"Maria!" the woman shouted back into the little adobe house. "Is the doctor finished?"

A tired male voice answered in Spanish. "I am just finished. What do you wish of Maria? I gave her a sleeping powder and ordered her to stay in bed for the day."

The man to whom the voice belonged appeared next to the woman at the door. To her, he said, "Your girls can clean up after me. I am tired. You're lucky I even came." When he realized she wasn't alone, but was with two Americans, his manner changed. In English, he said, "Good morning, gentlemen. If you please?"

Slocum and Jack parted, making way for the doctor,

black bag in hand, to exit the adobe. Again, Slocum asked, "Can we see her, please?"

The woman, who Slocum guessed to be the madam, gave a scowl, paused, then said, "Only if you pay." She held out her hand, palm up.

Slocum sighed, but he dipped fingers into his pocket and pulled out another gold coin, which he placed in her palm.

She stared at it. "It is real?" she asked, then bit it. She smiled, self-satisfied, then stepped back, making way for them to enter. "Down the hall. Third door on the right side."

Slocum was glad to be done with her. He was running out of Spanish, not to mention patience.

To Jack he said, "Maria's down the hall. The madam said she recognizes one'a Stevens's aliases, but she didn't actually see him for herself. If the doc's knockout stuff doesn't work too fast, Maria can take a look at the picture."

Excitement had overtaken Jack again. He rubbed his hands together anxiously.

Slocum muttered, "Knock it off," without breaking stride until he reached the third door on the right. He knocked.

From within, he heard someone female mutter groggily, *"Sí?"*

In Spanish, Slocum asked if they might come in and speak with her. She said yes, and in they went.

She was a tiny thing, and beautiful, with long black-brown hair that lay loose on the pillow as she reclined, staring out the window. Her left forearm had just been cast in plaster of Paris, and still glinted damply. *"Sí?"* she asked before she turned her head to look at them. Fear suddenly overtook her features, and she whispered, *"Gringos!"*

Right away, Slocum held up his hands to show that they were empty. "Miss Lopez?" he asked in English.

"Yes?" she answered in kind, although somewhat shakily.

"You speak English?" Jack asked hopefully.

"A little," she replied, looking past them toward the door. Probably for help, Slocum thought.

"Miss Lopez, I'm hoping you can help us," he said. "We're lookin' to find this man." He held out the poster of Wall Stevens.

She didn't need to answer. Her reaction—which was to shrink back and cover her mouth—said it for her.

Slocum sat on the side of her bed. "It's all right now, Maria," he said, his voice soothing. "It's all right. We're looking to arrest him."

Her eyes went to Slocum's face. "He . . . he has done this before?"

"Yes, and much, much worse. Is he still in town?"

"He had no plans to leave. He is staying at the Cantina Blanca," she said, and then she nodded her head toward the north. "Saltillo, at the corner of Third Street. He is dangerous?"

"He has killed many men," Slocum said gravely.

"You *señors* will do me the honor of a favor?" She looked back and forth, from Slocum to Jack and back again. "You will blacken his eye and break his arm for me?"

Before Jack could answer with an enthusiastic "Yes!"— and he was most likely to do just that—Slocum said, "I think the Territory of Arizona will more than oblige you, Maria. He's wanted dead or alive, and that means they're sure to hang him, no matter what."

This seemed to satisfy her. Also, Slocum figured the medication was kicking in. She turned away from them and lay on her right side. "Thank you, miss," Slocum said softly, slipped two double eagles under her pillow, and stood up. Jack on his heels, he went back up the hall and out the front door.

Immediately, Jack practically shouted, "We got 'im now! Oh boy, we surely got 'im!"

Slocum was just plain disgusted by this time. He snarled, "You always celebrate before your birthday, too?"

"Oh," said Jack. "Sorry. You always pay that much for information? You gave her forty dollars!"

"Quiet! You want that madam to hear and take it away from her?"

Jack blinked. "Oh. Sorry."

They mounted up and set off for the Cantina Blanca.

10

Cantina Blanca was set along Saltillo Street with a barber's shop on one side, and a string of other businesses—a grocer, a textiles shop, a hardware, etc.—on the other. Unlike the other buildings, however, it had a second story. Slocum figured that Stevens was staying up there, if he was still in town.

He and Jack dismounted and tied their horses, while Slocum said, "Listen, Jack, if you know what's good for you, you'll act normal. Keep your hands away from your guns. Smile. Okay?"

"Okay," came the sluggish reply. Then, "You sure know how to take all the fun outta this, Slocum."

He turned toward Jack and said, "I'm just tryin' to keep you alive. Now mind."

The two men entered the cantina, and Slocum paused beside the door for a moment, scanning the scant crowd. No Stevens in sight. Next, he walked up to the bar and asked the barkeep if he knew the man on the poster. The bartender nodded and informed them—well, Slocum anyway—that he was staying in a room upstairs, but that he was out for the moment.

In Spanish, Slocum told the bartender just who Stevens really was, and not to let on that they'd spoken with him. He was to just act normally. They would take care of the rest.

The bartender agreed—more enthusiastically when Slocum slipped him a ten-dollar gold piece—and Slocum led Jack to a rear table, where they sat down.

Slocum signaled the barkeep. *"Dos cervezas, por favor."* Then to Jack, he said, "Might's well have a drink before we get ourselves killed."

Jack made a face. "Stop it. We been real lucky so far. What makes you figure our luck's gonna change?"

"Luck ain't got nothin' to do with it, Jack. Remember that. It's keepin' the upper hand, always. Thinkin' ahead of your man. Bein' ready for anythin', 'cause anything can happen."

Jack didn't answer, because just then, the barkeep brought their drinks. Jack sat there, his fingers loosely through the handle on the mug, swinging it in slow circles over the damp tabletop. Finally, he said, "If you say so."

Slocum nodded and took the first draw on his beer. It was warm and watery, but it still tasted good. Stevens had found a nice place to hole up. He'd bet cash money that no one had so much as thought about looking for him down here. And that was including the sheriff. They—town sheriffs, that was—mostly figured that they had enough to do already, and that the Mexicans could take care of themselves.

Slocum patted his pockets until he found the one with the playing cards in it, then pulled them out. "Might's well play a hand or two of poker while we wait. Okay?"

Jack perked up a little. "Sure."

Slocum began to shuffle and asked, "Five-card draw fine by you?"

Jack nodded, and Slocum began to deal. The front doors swung open, letting in a fan of light, and Slocum's eyes barely flicked up. A tad more loudly than usual, he said, "Sure wish we had a third man. More of a game that way."

Jack lifted his gaze to meet Slocum's, and nodded. He got the picture. Good.

Both men sat back and opened their cards. "Bet a dime," said Jack.

"Well, you're just Mr. Money Bags, ain't you?" Slocum said with a chuckle. "I'll see that and raise you a nickel." He flipped two coins out on the tabletop.

Jack saw the raise, and then it was Slocum's turn. "How many cards?"

Jack pursed his lips, then lay three of his hand cards facedown on the table. "Three," he said, and Slocum dealt them out.

"And dealer takes one." Slocum dealt himself one card. "Your bet." Casually, he looked up. Right into the face of Wall Stevens. "Well, I'll be damned!" he said with a grin on his face. "Another American! What brings you to the Mexican quarter, brother?"

Stevens, a short, dark-haired man with slicked back hair and manicured nails, said, "The tortillas. And you ain't my brother."

Slocum waved his hands, showing that they were empty. "Sorry, sorry, no offense meant." He held out a hand. "I'm Slocum, and this here's my partner, Jack Tandy. Care to have a hand with us? The beer's on me."

Stevens wavered, and for a moment, Slocum thought he was going to lose him. But then he said, "Sure. Why the hell not?"

He pulled out a chair to Slocum's left and sat down.

Slocum signaled the barkeep again. *"Una mas, por favor!"* He grinned at Stevens. "We're just in the middle of a hand, here . . ."

Jack said, "No, we're not." He put down his cards. "You're dealin' junk."

"All right, smart ass, you deal." Slocum handed him the cards. He turned toward Stevens. "And what should we be callin' you, friend?"

With no hesitation, Stevens replied, "It's Mel. Mel Stevens." He tipped his head toward Jack, who was busy shuffling the cards. "You sure this is a friendly game?"

Slocum grinned. "Friendly as it gets, Mel. Hey, Jack, you gonna deal those before you get the numbers worn right off of 'em?"

"Ah, hold your horses," Jack said, then began to deal. "Five-card stud. Jacks or better to open. Ante's a quarter."

If he had kept talking just a little longer, Slocum would've had time to pull his gun and buffalo Stevens. But no such luck. They had to play out the hand and let the deal go to Stevens.

When it did, Stevens was in midshuffle when Slocum slipped his left gun from its holster, flipped it in midair, and buffaloed him alongside the temple. He went down right away, of course, and Slocum holstered his gun before saying to Jack, "You get his feet." With Jack on one end and Slocum on the other, they got Stevens's inert form outside and, after asking the bartender, got him on the right horse. She was a pretty little sorrel—too pretty for the likes of Stevens to own, Slocum thought.

Once again, Jack was almost unbearable on their way up to the jail. He shut up, though, when the sheriff told them that Stevens's bounty had gone up since the poster came out. It was now five thousand dollars, which Jack—who, according to his story, had practically taken Stevens all on his own—magnanimously split with Slocum.

Slocum was the last one out of the office, and overheard the sheriff mutter, "Cocky little shithead . . ." as he closed the door.

Slocum had to smile.

Jack, already mounted, asked, "What it is?"

"Nothin'," replied Slocum, still grinning. "Not a damn thing." He mounted up, too, and they set off for the bank to deposit their vouchers.

"And then what did he say?" a laughing Katie asked. "Lord, I wish I'd been there!" She was getting such a kick out of Slocum's retelling of the morning's story that she'd had to excuse herself twice to go to the outhouse, lest she embarrass herself.

"That was it," Slocum said, although he wasn't enjoying her level of enthusiasm. "We just got on the horses and went to the bank. The end." He sat back in his chair.

Katie wiped at her eyes. "Well, my goodness, if I'd known that your takin' up bounty huntin' was gonna be this much fun, I would'a insisted you take it up years ago!" She blew her nose. "What a hoot!"

Flatly, he said, "Glad somebody enjoyed it."

She rose from the kitchen table, kissed him on the forehead, and said, "Sounds to me like somebody needs to cut loose from his partner."

Slocum dug in his pocket for his fixings bag. "Yup. Just got to figure out how to do it kindly, like. And how to do it so he don't try to go off and bounty hunt on his own."

Katie lifted a brow in an unspoken question, and Slocum added, "Because he's likely to get himself killed, that's why!"

"That bad?"

Slocum lit his quirlie, then nodded. "That bad."

She reached into the cupboard for an ashtray and slid it toward him.

"Thanks," he said, shaking out his lucifer.

She leaned back against the counter and folded her arms. "Well, we need to find out what he can do—and do well— and hope to God it's somethin' he likes."

Through a haze of exhaled smoke, he replied, "He likes ranch work, but I sure wouldn't lay money on him in Apache territory. Best find him somethin' he can do in town. He's got almost six grand in the bank."

"Seems to me he could buy himself a business of some kind with that much cash." Katie poured herself a cup of coffee. "He could buy a house and a buggy and a herd of cattle, too! Nobody ever told me he was rich. How'd he like to invest in a nice little whorehouse?"

Slocum burst out laughing. "Avaricious little wench, aren't you?"

"Never claimed not to be. Want coffee?"

"Wouldn't mind. Anybody gonna eat that last piece of apple pie?"

"Thought you'd never ask," she said, and pushed the pie tin and a fork toward him, along with his coffee. "Wanna finish off the whipped cream for me, too?"

He smiled wide. "How'd you know?"

Later that evening, after Slocum and Katie had gone to bed— and after they'd both come twice—she was curled beneath one of his strong arms when she suddenly smacked herself on the forehead and said, "Oh, I *am* a dolt!"

Slocum sat up straight, taking Katie along with him, and asked, "What? What? Why are you a dolt?" He thought she'd suddenly taken leave of her senses.

"Rance Cooney, that's why! He was in here the other

night, sayin' as how he was gonna have to leave Phoenix and go back East!"

Slocum turned her to face him. "Katie, what on earth are you talkin' about?"

"Rance Cooney owns the hardware, over on Fifth," she explained, like she was talking to an idiot. "It's for sale!" When Slocum stared at her dumbly, she jabbed him in the ribs with her elbow. "For Jack! He know anything about the hardware business?"

Slocum said, "I dunno, but it's worth findin' out, ain't it?"

Katie laughed. "It sure is! I don't know what he's askin', but I know he does landslide business over there."

"Good girl, Katie," he said with a grin. "Smart girl, too!"

She lay back down and grinned. "I have my moments."

"You sure do." His grin widened. "Y'know, I've been known to have some pretty good ideas, myself. On occasion." He turned and lowered himself over her.

"You have?" she whispered playfully.

He moved gently from side to side, his chest just touching her upturned nipples. "Every once in a while."

"Give me an example, please?"

"Happy to," he said, bringing first one knee, then the other, between hers, and nudging them apart. "But I'd rather show you."

He eased into her warmth, and she let out a long sigh as he did.

"I'm beginning to get the picture, Mr. Slocum. Please, elucidate?"

He did, with gusto.

11

In the morning, while he waited for Jack to rub the sleep out of his eyes, Slocum sat at the kitchen table and spread out the posters before him. As luck would have it, they'd already taken in the highest-paying men on the list. All that was left were the penny-ante players, all paying in the hundreds, not the thousands.

His eye lit on one poster. He was pretty sure he'd seen the face before, in one of the saloons two days past. He hadn't paid any mind, since he was hunting for bigger quarry, and ignored it. But today, he remembered. He also remembered that the man in question had turned his back as soon as Slocum pulled out the poster and asked if the bartender recognized the picture.

A piece of cake, he thought, just as Jack stumbled in and slumped down in a chair. Slocum said, "Good morning?"

Jack raised his head and said, through a fringe of uncombed hair, "Yeah. I s'pose. They got any coffee hottened up?"

Slocum allowed that they did, indeed, and got up to fetch a cup and the pot. If he could talk Jack into this, his troubles would be over, and Jack would be the proud new owner of a hardware store. Or whatever took his fancy.

After Jack inhaled his first cup and poured his second, Slocum said, "I think I found us another one."

Jack's brows shot up. "Where? Here?"

"It was the day before yesterday. I think I saw him while we were askin' questions up at the Purple Garter Saloon."

"Well, why didn't you say somethin'? We could'a got two for one!"

"'Cause he wasn't the man we were lookin' for. I just now remembered his face." He pointed to the poster. The man in question was probably forty years old, had gray hair and a mustache, and was named Silas Recker. He was wanted for a number of petty crimes—quite a number, in fact—and was worth four hundred dollars. "He ain't worth much, but four hundred's better than nothin'."

"When do we go get him?" Jack was already halfway out of the chair.

Slocum shot out a hand and pushed him back down. "First, you get some grub into you. And second, you're doin' this one on your own."

"I am?" Curiosity replaced Jack's surprise. "Why come?"

"I just figger you could use the practice. And I don't think he's much likely to draw on you. But if he does, don't kill him. He ain't worth a blamed cent if you do."

Jack nodded. "Okay. I guess. But wouldn't you rather be there? You know, to see?"

What he meant was *to back me up,* but Slocum wasn't falling for it. Jack needed a little taste of what he was really doing. Or pretending to do.

Slocum said, "I'll be outside, waitin' for you to come out, and I'll help you get him down to the sheriff's office.

All right? But if you can take him alone, the money's all yours. Then again, he might not be there. Might be someplace else."

"Where?"

"You're the bounty hunter. You're supposed to find that out." Slocum took another sip of his own coffee.

Jack looked downright dejected for a minute or so, then stiffened his backbone. "All right. I'm game."

Slocum leaned back in his chair. "There's part of a coffee cake under the dishtowel on the sideboard's counter."

It was around noon when the two men got to the Purple Garter—just about the same time they'd been there yesterday, Slocum reckoned. Jack got a little shakier with every block they walked, but each time Slocum asked if he was sure he wanted to do this, he got a nod in reply. Well, let the chips fall where they may, then.

Outside, Slocum pulled up a bench. Saying, "See you later. And remember, no shootin'," he began to roll a quirlie. Out of the corner of his eye, he saw Jack pause at the batwing doors, take himself a deep breath, then go inside.

Slocum leaned back. Actually, he didn't expect Recker to be in there. He'd probably switched saloons or left town yesterday. Slocum figured it was going to be long day, but it'd be worth it if Jack saw how much legwork and question asking—usually of people who didn't wish to answer any— bounty hunting actually entailed.

Not that Slocum was any authority. But he'd been around, seen and done things that Jack Tandy hadn't even dreamt of.

To Slocum's way of thinking, this was breaking in the kid gently.

He had planned to take a hike up to the tobacconist's after he finished his quirlie, while Jack made his fruitless search of the Purple Garter. He liked a good cigar, and he wanted to have one today if all he was going to do was follow Jack around.

But he had no more than touched his quirlie with a flaming sulphur tip when all hell broke loose inside.

Suddenly the soft clink of glasses and the occasional hum of conversation or bubble of laughter were replaced by the sounds of chairs crashing, tables being knocked over, men being punched—and gunfire!

"Oh, you little idiot!" Slocum snarled as he jumped to his feet and ran inside.

The battle finished as suddenly as it had started, and what greeted Slocum inside, amid some battered furniture, was a passel of men standing around—some with bloody noses, some with bruised lips or jaws or blackened eyes—at the edges of the saloon. In the center of it all stood Jack—unarmed—and Recker, flat on his ass on the floor.

Behind him, Slocum heard the cock of a shotgun and twisted toward it in time to see the barkeep leveling a double-barreled shotgun and hear him shout, "I said, knock it off, you bunch'a shitheads! Look at the mess you peckerwoods done made, and just when I got it put together from the last time!"

Recker made a grab for his gun, but the barkeep fired a round over his head, and Recker dropped the pistol as if it had just come out of the oven.

"The idiot's always got somebody to help him out," Slocum mumbled beneath his breath, and moved forward.

"All right," he announced to the crowd. "Everybody mind the barkeep and get back outta the way. Silas Recker, consider yourself under arrest. I'm takin' you in for numerous counts of petty larceny and robbery and such. On your feet now. Jack, you get his pistol."

Jack let out a huge breath of air and scrambled toward Silas's gun. Silas looked pissed, and he likely had plenty of right. It was likely that his day wasn't going according to plan either.

"You're takin' in ol' Silas?" asked a man across the room. "Why, he never hurt a fly!"

"Mebbe not, but he stole a few," Slocum replied. "Your prisoner, Jack. Best get him on down to the sheriff's office."

"Yessir!" Jack answered, just a little too happily, and wiggled the nose of Silas Recker's own pistol in the older man's face. "Hands behind your head, fingers locked." When Silas grudgingly complied, Jack said, "Good. Now, let's get on down to the jail, Silas."

At least he'd remembered the thing about the hands locked behind the man's head, Slocum thought. Maybe there was some hope for him after all.

A long and tiresome explanation of exactly what had happened down at the Purple Garter followed at the sheriff's office, and Slocum was relieved he hadn't asked any questions on the way there. About forty minutes of this was all he could stand.

Jack kept trying to make himself out a hero, but the sheriff questioned everything he said. The prisoner disagreed with his story at every turn, too, and then Wall Stevens kicked in with his two cents' worth, and then Tom Mitchell had to start yammering, too.

If it had taken Jack only a quarter of the time to "capture" Silas Recker than he was taking to tell the story, then they'd still be up at the saloon, Slocum thought.

Through the noise of all of them ringing in his ears, Slocum suddenly stood straight up and yelled, "Quiet!"

Amazingly, the jail was suddenly silent.

"Sheriff," he went on, "you got your man locked up in the cell over there. Just give Jack here the voucher and let's be done with it. All right?"

The sheriff agreed, and Slocum sent Jack on up to the bank with his voucher. Shit. The kid was as cocky as ever. Slocum would have liked to get his hands on that bartender. He figured that if he couldn't get it away from him, at least he could bump him so that his final shot was a little lower.

Just a wound, Lord, he prayed. *Just a simple flesh wound is all I ask . . .*

He settled back in the armchair in Katie's room and lit the cigar he'd picked up on the way home. He was alone, Katie having gone out before he showed up, to run some errands.

The cigar didn't taste right, and he blamed this on Jack, too. He'd been blaming Jack for everything from the weather to the parlor drapes all the way from the sheriff's office. What was with that kid anyway?

No, stop that shit, he thought. *He ain't no goddamn kid. You were younger than him when the war was over and done. He's just green as hell, that's all.*

And green could be a dangerous thing.

Slocum figured that he'd best get shed of Jack as soon as possible. But yet, he didn't want to crush any real bravery that might pound in that chest of his. He thought there was some there—Jack just hadn't called it up yet.

He rolled his ash off in the little crystal ashtray that Katie kept on her table, and settled back again. What the hell to do now? Jack would likely come back from the bank all cocky and full of himself, and raring to go after their next quarry.

Well, they'd have to head north to find the next one. At least he was good company on the trail, Slocum thought. But that didn't make up for much, when you came right down to it.

A man who could do the job was what he needed, and Jack constantly proved he wasn't that man.

Then again, why did he need anybody? Slocum had ridden alone for most of the years since the war. If this was going to be his new line of work—and a well-paying line it was—why was he so ready to take on a partner at this late date? He thought back, back to Tucson, and tried to remember how he'd gotten tangled up with this pup in the first place.

"Damn it, I'm too softhearted!" he said aloud, announcing a trait that he'd never been accused of owning. Well, except when it came to horses.

But he'd been softhearted and softheaded, too. He'd been impressed that Jack had the balls to try and take him in for that old Tucson misunderstanding, for one thing. And when he realized that good money could be made by rounding up badasses—most of whom were no badder than he was—Jack just happened to be around.

And there it was. Well, what was done could be undone, if not quite so easily. He rolled the ash off his cigar again, and glanced out the window.

Someone once said, *Think of the devil and he shall appear.* And there was Jack, just coming up the walk. Grinning like a shit-eating dog, of course.

He was practically skipping.

12

Slocum waited until after supper to talk to Jack. It took him that long to cool off after he saw Jack come skipping home. By that time, he had his temper under control—well, as "under control" as it could be, considering the circumstances—and thought that if Jack could level with him, then he could level with Jack.

He figured that was downright generous. What Jack thought? That remained to be seen.

When they shoved back from the dinner table, full as ticks, Slocum asked to join him on the front porch for a smoke. Jack readily agreed, especially since he had a couple of expensive hand-rolled, port-soaked cigars figuratively burning a hole in his pocket.

They sat down on the porch swing, and Jack offered Slocum the spare cigar. Slocum took it and lit up, then shared the match with Jack. It'd make this a tad more pleasant. Well, civilized anyway.

"Jack," began Slocum, "I think we oughta talk."

"'Bout what?"

Amazed, Slocum slowly turned toward him. "You don't even know you did anything wrong, do you?"

Jack's eyebrows bunched, then arched. "Wrong? What are you talkin' about?"

Calmly—well, calmly for Slocum—he began to elucidate. At length.

When he was finished, all the cocky was washed out of Jack. A couple of times, Slocum thought he was going to burst into tears, and had to change the subject slightly, or steer it in a new direction.

But he got through it, and so did Jack. Slocum was fairly certain that Jack was permanently convinced never to lie to the sheriff again and to quit the self-puffery. If he wanted to pursue this line of work, there were going to have to be a lot of changes made. Or on the other hand, he'd heard of a nice business property that was for sale there in town.

Unfortunately, the hardware store news slid off him like water off a duck's back, but the warnings about his behavior in the bounty hunting trade seemed to take better hold. That was some comfort, but Slocum would have been a lot happier if Jack had suddenly jumped to his feet at the mention of the hardware store, and shouted, "That's for me!"

No such luck, though.

Well, Slocum would take what he could get at this point. And, he had to admit, the cigar was good.

"You know," he said, "I still ain't satisfied that you can handle things on your own. I believe we'll take us a little trip in the mornin' and try again. You game?"

"Sure I am!"

Dumb enthusiasm, thy name is Jack Tandy, Slocum thought, and barely resisted the urge to just smack Jack across the face. No, he'd let life do that, and he was certain it would. Eventually.

Slocum stood up. "Believe I'll go in now. Coffee's callin'."

Jack stood up as well. "Believe I'll go in with you a ways, but I'm turnin' at the stairs." He winked.

"How much is this costin' you?" Slocum wasn't getting charged a red cent, but Jack was another matter entirely.

"I dropped about three hundred so far."

"What?!"

Jack broke out laughing. "I'm just foolin' with you, buddy. Less'n half that."

"A hundred an' fifty is still a whole helluva lot of money. You'd best be savin' that for your future." Slocum thumped his forehead with the heel of his palm. "Sorry. I don't mean to sound like somebody's father." Jack must've been at it like a rabbit to run up that bill. He'd talk to Katie.

"And that's what happened, according to him," Slocum finished up. Katie'd sat through the whole telling, rapt and wide-eyed, but with one eyebrow cocked, which told Slocum that she had her doubts.

She sat back and folded her arms. "And you're sure he's tellin' the truth?"

Slocum shrugged. If he couldn't count on his partner telling him the truth, then he couldn't count on anybody. Jack had put him between a rock and a hard place, and now Katie was pushing on the rock. He tried changing the subject. "He also told me that he's dropped around a hundred and fifty bucks in here so far. That the truth?"

Katie scowled. "I should say not! Not unless Jasmine's holdin' out on me, and she wouldn't do that. She's a good girl, and she has genuine feelings for that little liar. A hundred and fifty, my ass! It's more like fifty, tops."

Now it was Slocum's turn to arch his brows. Fifty? That damn sonofabitch lied about everything! Or had he just exaggerated to make himself seem more important, more manly?

"Fifty?" he said aloud. "I gotta get rid of Jack, and that's it."

"I should say you do," said Katie.

"Except we're heading up north tomorrow."

"What? Why?"

"Because if I just tell him to go away, I'll never get shed of him."

"That why you sent him into the saloon alone today?"

"Right. He needs to get his butt whipped all on his lonesome. He needs to figure this out for himself. Mind if I finish my cigar?"

"Not so long as you bring the ashtray over here," she said, and smiled. She was sitting, cross-legged, in bed at the time.

Slocum gave a halfhearted grin and got up, the springs squeaking, fetched the ashtray, and came back. He perched on the edge of the mattress while he dug out what was left of his cigar, scratched a lucifer into flame, and lit his smoke.

He took a draw on it. One thing about Jack—he knew how to pick a good cigar. It sure didn't make up for the other stuff, though, Slocum thought. He felt a small, cool hand on his shoulder.

"Why don't you lean back and relax, and tell me what you plan to do up north," Katie purred.

Slocum sighed and gave in to gravity. "I think we can find Rupert Grimes up there, somewhere around Russian Chimes."

Katie looked surprised. "I didn't know there was anything or anybody left in Russian Chimes! You're going to a ghost town?"

Slocum shook his head. "No, I said somewhere *around*

there. Ol' Rupert ain't worth much, and he's never been known to use a gun, but he might be good for wearin' down our Jack."

"He's not *my* Jack. Don't you go blamin' him on me."

Katie had that resolute look on her face, which meant she wasn't about to be talked into—or out of—anything. And Slocum had no intention of trying either.

He said, "Now, Katie, you know I didn't mean it like that. He's not your problem, he's mine. I hope to God that this'll take care of him for good and all."

She nodded. "More like it. I wish you luck."

He puffed on his cigar. "Thanks. I'm gonna need it. Seems like the little shit always finds somebody to fix it so that he comes out smellin' like a rose."

"And you'd rather he came out smellin' like cow pies?"

"Exactly!" Slocum threw his arm around her shoulders.

Katie sighed. "Men," she said, resigned. "I'll never understand how that brain'a yours works."

"You come closer than any woman I've ever met, Katie-bird. That's a compliment, in case you were wonderin'."

"Figured it was." She gave her head a slow shake. "Slocum?"

"What?"

"Are we done with talkin' for a while?"

"I reckon," he replied through a cloud of smoke.

"Then, can we do somethin' else?"

"Like what?" he asked before he realized they were in her bedroom, on her bed, and they were still fully clothed. "Oh!" he laughed, tickled by his own denseness. "Miss Katie, would you do me the great and glorious honor of strippin' off every last stitch of your clothes?"

"I would be delighted, Mr. Slocum. Will you please do the same?"

"De-lighted," he said, answering like one of those pompous old officers he remembered from the war years. "It would be my distinct pleasure, ma'am."

The next morning, Katie waved good-bye from the front yard as Slocum and Jack set out for the north. Of course, she had kissed and hugged Slocum and told him to watch his back—and for God's sake not to go to Texas—before he and Jack walked up to the stable. And he knew she meant every pet and every lip-lock of it. But she didn't need to worry, not really. This would be a piece of cake. He figured he could stir old Rupert Grimes out of the woodwork with no trouble, and bang, Jack'd get a lesson he wouldn't forget.

Jack groused occasionally for the first two or three miles of the ride, but then that was it. It probably helped when Slocum shot him a dirty look and said, "Shut the hell up, will you?"

Where they were headed, Russian Chimes, had been a mining town until the gold ran out about three years back. The last time Slocum had been through there, it was nothing but a ghost town, with half of the ramshackle-built structures falling in on themselves, and not a single soul around.

Outside the town, though, there were a few tiny pockets of what you could charitably call civilization. Lem Shingle used to live up there, about a mile out, with his family, eking out a scant living by farming and raising the occasional cow. Slocum liked old Lem. He hoped the Apache hadn't gotten him. Or his kids. What was that little gal's name? She couldn't have been more than sixteen the last time Slocum was through—but then, that had been two years or so ago. Pretty little thing, he recalled. Blond.

"How long's it take to get there?" Jack asked from behind him.

"We can get there before dark if we keep goin' like we been," Slocum replied. He knew that Jack's pinto wasn't the easiest to ride at a jog, so he added, "Come on. Let's lope for a spell."

Jack sprang forward—and Slocum thought he heard a muttered "Thank God" when Jack passed him, but he let Rocky have his head, and in no time he passed Jack.

They were going through pretty country. They gained in altitude all the time, but the grass was thick and green and broken by stray patches of cholla or prickly pear. Insects buzzed, birds sang and called, once they saw a small group of pronghorn in the distance, and not a single Apache was in sight. Or within hearing. Much to Slocum's surprise, it was turning into a pleasant ride.

Jack had stopped his griping, too. As they loped along, he was grinning like a kid, taking it all in. He had to have been this way before, Slocum thought. He'd said he'd worked in Prescott for a spell, hadn't he? Well, maybe he'd taken a different route down to Phoenix. If he'd followed the old Butterfield stage route down from Flagstaff, Slocum understood why he was appreciating this so much. He didn't care for that one so much himself.

He slowed Rocky down to a jog, then a walk, and signaled Jack to do the same. "Let's let the horses walk for about half an hour, and then we'll stop and eat," he said.

Jack nodded and grinned.

Katie had packed them a big sack of grub, which was tied behind Slocum's saddle, and they were both anxious to see what was in it.

13

They stopped at a quiet spot, took care of the horses, and then broke into Katie's bag with great anticipation.

And it was worth the wait. Inside, Slocum found half a roasted chicken, a packet of roast beef, sliced and ready to be made into sandwiches with the half a loaf of fresh bread she'd included. There was a bowl of potato salad, too, and half an apple pie! They were in hog heaven, especially when Slocum announced that they'd hit their goal in time for supper.

So Jack made himself a thick roast beef sandwich, pulled off a couple of pieces of roasted chicken, and took half the potato salad, to boot. Slocum figured what the hell, and aped him. He noted that all during lunch, Jack kept eyeing the apple pie, to the point where Slocum had to say, "Jack, the pie ain't goin' nowhere. It ain't got legs, y'know."

Jack grinned sheepishly and kept on eating.

And that boy could surely eat! Slocum figured that he

must have three or four stomachs, like a cow, to put away
that much chuck that fast!

They finally made it to the pie, and Slocum decided to
make things simple. He just cut the thing in half, took his,
and handed the other half to Jack. He went through it like
beets through a baby's backside, and sat back, licking his
lips, before Slocum was halfway finished with his.

Slocum made a point of eating slowly, relishing every
bite, while Jack sat and watched, empty-handed. Katie had
once teasingly accused him of gobbling his food down like
a farm animal, but she had yet to see Jack eat after a long
morning's ride. Slocum figured she'd have to set a whole
new standard after witnessing that!

They set off again on full stomachs, growing ever closer
to their goal. They wouldn't ride into Russian Chimes itself, not today anyhow. Lem Shingle's place was just south
of the old town, which meant they'd come to it first. And it
couldn't have come at a better time for Slocum. Jack's
pinto mare was almost in full-blown season, and Rocky had
been strutting his stuff all day. Well, the long lope had taken
some of that out of him, but he was still eager to get to her.
If anyone but Slocum had been riding him, he wouldn't
have hesitated to mount her even while Jack was in her
saddle.

However, he was doing a good job of minding his p's
and q's, and so far hadn't even shoved his nose up her
rump. He hoped Lem would have some way to put them up
separately.

Some good *sound* way.

It was just about five in the afternoon when they rode
up to Lem's doorstep. Slocum saw that he'd put a barn up
in the two years since he'd visited there, and built an addition to the house as well. Well, you couldn't call Lem a
slacker, that was for sure.

They rode nearly up to the front door before it opened, and Lem came out, carrying a rifle. But when he saw it was Slocum, he let the rifle swing nose-down and gave out a shout. "Mother!" he called. "It's Slocum, come to visit!"

Slocum returned Lem's grin and swung down off Rocky. The two men shook hands and hugged and pounded each other's backs. Lem had saved Slocum from a grizzly bear long ago, but Slocum had never forgotten it: the stench of the bear's roar, the power of her paw as she just swept him aside like so much kindling, and her weight as she fell on him. It was Lem's bullet that had taken her down and saved Slocum from being eaten alive, and suffering only a couple of broken ribs.

He reached over and gave Lem an extra sideways hug, for good measure. And for helping him to get out from under the bear as well! Hell, he'd still be there today if it hadn't been for Lem. He'd just be an unknown skeleton of an unknown man pinned beneath the bones of an unknown grizzly, somewhere in the Rocky Mountains.

Lem seemed to know what he was thinking, and laughed. "You still wrasslin' that bear, Slocum?"

Slocum flushed. "Well, maybe . . ."

Lem laughed again. "And who's this fine young man?" he asked, nodding toward Jack.

Jack said, "What bear?"

Slocum ignored him and said, "Lem, like you to meet my travelin' companion, Jack Tandy. Jack, Lem."

Jack moved forward and held out his hand for Lem to shake, which he did. Just then, Martha came out, drying her hands on an old dishtowel. "Oh, Slocum!" she cried and ran into his arms, hugging him like she'd thought she'd never see him again.

Lem's face got a little stiff, and Slocum laughed. Lem was well aware of his reputation with the ladies, and every

time he got within ten miles of Martha, Lem suddenly remembered it. But Martha was safe. She was as short and
round as he was tall and thin, was a wonderful cook, and
had a bubbly laugh as effervescent as she was good-hearted.
But she knew a scalawag when she met one, and she'd pegged
Slocum right off.

That didn't mean she didn't like him, though.

She stood back at arm's length, shook her head, and
smiling, said, "Well, look what the cat dragged in, Lemuel!
I swan, I never thought we'd see you again, Slocum. What
brings you up this way, and who's your handsome young
friend?"

Slocum introduced Jack again, then explained their
mission—as much as he could in front of Jack, that was.
Lem scratched his chin whiskers for a moment, thinking.
Or at least Slocum hoped he was thinking.

And then he said, "Can I see a picture of this feller?"

Slocum dug through his pockets for Rupert Grimes's
poster, and handed it over. Lem studied it for a moment,
holding it out at arm's length and squinting, then said,
"Mother, isn't this the new feller that Sandy hired on?"

Martha moved to look. She cocked her head. "Might
be," she allowed. "It's not a very good drawing, is it?"

"This Sandy," said Slocum. "How far away's his place?"

"On the other side'a Russian Chimes," said Lem, nodding back toward the east. "I can take ya, iff'n you want."

"No need, Lem. Just directions, that's all we want."

Lem was looking past him. "You'd best be wantin' a
place to confine your friend's mare, too."

Rocky was dancing on the end of his reins. Slocum said,
"It'd sure take a load off my mind, Lem. Rocky's been dan-
cin' the polka all day."

Lem laughed. "You still got that sense'a humor, Slocum.
C'mon, Jack. I got a nice vacant stall where you can put

your mare up for the night." He started toward the barn, and Jack followed him, leading his pinto.

Rocky tried to follow, but Slocum pulled him back. "She's not your type, big fella," he said, and smiled. "Sorry."

He turned back toward Martha. "So where's that little girl of yours?"

Martha smiled. "Where you can't get your hands on her, Slocum. She's back East, at finishing school. And I plan on keepin' her there so long as you keep comin' around."

"Oh, now, Martha, I was lookin' forward to seein' her again. She was a cute little button!"

"Uh-huh."

"Why Martha, you got a dirty mind!" Slocum said, raising his eyebrows as he feigned surprise—and also innocence.

"That's the pot callin' the kettle black," she responded with a laugh. "Go settle your stud in the corral, then come inside for some vittles. I just put on a couple'a extra venison steaks for you and your friend. And glory hallelujah, we got ketchup this year. The tomatoes come up awful good."

"Sounds great, Martha! I'll be right in!"

Later, Slocum and Jack pushed back from the table, full as ticks. Martha had made coleslaw and fried potatoes to go with the venison, and there was cake for dessert!

"Mind if I smoke?" Slocum asked, his fixings bag halfway out of his pocket.

"Have I ever?" asked Martha.

"No, ma'am, I don't believe you have," Slocum replied, and began to roll himself a quirlie. Lem had already filled his pipe and lit it, and he leaned back in his chair with a satisfied ear-to-ear grin on his face.

He said, "Mother, that was one fine meal," and Slocum and Jack, who had already voiced their gratitude for such tasty bounty, grunted and nodded their agreement. "Now, Slocum," he went on, "just what is it that this feller has did that you're willin' to track him up here to arrest him? Seems to me you know what it's like to be on the other end'a that sort'a deal."

Slocum was ready for him. He said, "Lem, I have had what they call a change of heart about the thievin' and rustlin' game. And Jack here is in trainin' to be my partner."

Jack took some exception to that last bit, but Slocum stilled him before he had a chance to stick his foot in his mouth. He went on, "I ain't wanted in Arizona, so it seemed like a good place to start out."

Lem nodded sagely, with his pipe clamped between his teeth. He plucked it out long enough to ask, "So, he ain't done nothin' personal to you, then."

Slocum shrugged his shoulders. "Not s'far as I know. He's bilked a lotta folks outta their money, though, money they'd saved up all their lives to buy ranches and such."

"And a bunch of other things, too!" broke in Jack.

Slocum nodded.

"He's the one who's been doin' that?" Lem suddenly sat forward.

Slocum eyed him. "Why? That stuff goin' on around here?"

"Hell and damnation! Slocum, last winter a buckboard full'a elephant seekers and their rug rats pulled up outside my front door and demanded I vacate *their* ranch! They had a bill'a sale and everythin'. I had to go and get the sheriff up at Strawberry in on it, and it went all the way to Prescott before they finally convinced them jackass settlers that they'd been rooked."

"Now, Lem," soothed Martha, "they thought they were in the right."

Lem dismissed her with a wave of his hand. "I don't care what they thought. This here's our land, period, been that way since '65. I lost two sons to it, buried right out there. I fought Injuns for it, and the big cattle ranchers, too, and I knew damn well it didn't belong to nobody but me and Martha. And that's the truth of it."

Slocum leaned forward, planted his elbows on the table, and shook his head. "Lem, I'm truly sorry for your troubles. I didn't know—elsewise you know I would'a been here."

Lem nodded, his wrath spent. "I know you would, Slocum. You always been a good and true friend to me, ain't he, Mother?"

"Yes, Lemuel," Martha replied soothingly.

"See? Mother agrees, so I know I'm in the right."

Slocum couldn't think of a damned thing to say, so he just nodded. Finally, he asked, "Why'd you ask, Lem? I mean, about why I was trackin' him?"

"Nothin'. Just curious, that's all. I mean, I don't believe you never done anything in your life without a damned good reason, and I guess this one's no different." He took another puff on his pipe. "Now you, young feller," he said to Jack, "I got me a dandy bay gelding out in that barn, you see him?"

Jack nodded.

"Good. 'Cause tomorrow, you're gonna be ridin' him. You just let that pinto mare of yours stay in the barn until she's outta season, and everybody'll breathe a little easier. All right? He reins good, got snake sense, and he's like ridin' butter at the jog."

Jack was pleased. He grinned and said, "You bet it's all right!"

"That's settled, then," Lem announced with a smile. He

climbed to his feet and moved from the table to a stuffed chair beside the fire. "I like t'end my day with a little quiet time an' a book. You fellers do what you want. You know where the sleeping quarters is, don't you, Slocum?"

"I sure do. Thanks again, Lem."

14

The next morning, Slocum found himself and Jack following Lem down what was left of a rutted road, going toward Russian Chimes. The town had been christened by an influx of Russian miners passing through, who stopped to wait out a snowstorm. They didn't know that snowstorms were rare here, and named the town in hope. They found the gold, too, and cleaned out every last nugget and flake before they moved on.

But they left behind a sort of a town, hastily and shabbily built, and now falling in on itself. As the men rode down the main—and only—street, they passed the ruined stable, an adobe mercantile gone to crumble and melt, and the whorehouse, its once brightly painted exterior peeling in the sun and its caved-in roof.

Slocum had a moment of sorrow. He had fond memories of that whorehouse, and the girls who used to ply their trade there. There had been a little Mexican gal . . . what was her name? Aw, hell. It had fallen right out of his head. But she was something, all right.

Constanza, that was it! Man, just when you stopped trying to remember . . . He smiled at himself.

The saloon was still mostly standing, he was pleased to see, the peeling name of it still illegible, being written in Russian. Slocum momentarily wondered if the proprietors had forgotten to take along any little bit of their wares. A half-bottle of whiskey hidden under the bar, perhaps, or an unfinished fifth in the back room.

He was thirsty and he knew Lem could use a drink, too. Slocum saw him throw a longing glance toward the old bar, too, but it didn't last. He led them on, straight down the middle of what was left of the street, with Slocum and Jack wordlessly, patiently following behind him.

They had left Russian Chimes behind now, and were traveling over hard, rocky territory. If Sandy Whatshisname was raising cattle on land like this, he was crazy. But then they crested the gentle rise they'd been climbing, and suddenly, everything was green. Cattle grazed in the valley beyond, and past that, smoke curled from the chimney of one of four buildings that Slocum could see.

As if Slocum had asked, Lem said, "This here's Sandy's spread. Goes up north a ways in the mountains and a full day's ride to the east. Yup, he got him a passel of good land for cattle, all right. And his name's Sandy Slade, if you were wonderin'."

Slocum nodded. "Yeah, I was. Thanks for the heads-up, Lem. Appreciate it."

Jack simply grunted.

They started down through increasingly greening grass toward the cattle and the buildings. Soon they were parting the cattle and riding through, and Slocum could make out more details up ahead. Corrals, an outhouse, two barns of moderate size, a shed, and of course, the ranch house. It wasn't large or showy, but even from this distance Slocum could see that it was pretty much Apache proofed.

There were gun ports, like those on a sea schooner, on the side of the house that Slocum could see. It was roofed in wood instead of thatch and thickly shingled. Out front, behind a wooden waist-high shield beneath another wooden roof, stood a Gatling gun, the kind that Slocum remembered from the war. Sandy Slade was more than ready for an Indian onslaught, all right.

Slocum was kind of afraid that Sandy would suddenly take them for Apache, and the Gatling gun would all of a sudden open up on them!

But it didn't, and they rode up into the yard at just about the time that the front door popped open and a sandy-haired, middle-aged man stepped out. "Howdy, Lem!" he called through his thick mustache. "Didya bring me some company?" He nodded toward Slocum and Jack.

"Sorta," said Lem as he dismounted. Slocum and Jack followed suit and swung down, too. "Sandy, like you to meet my good friend, Slocum, and his buddy, Jack."

Slocum stepped forward and shook hands with Sandy. "Pleased to meet you, Sandy." Jack, of course, was right behind him and shook Sandy's hand as well, but Sandy kept looking at Slocum.

"And the both of you," he said. "I heard a lot about you, Slocum. Lem talks you up all the time."

Slocum grinned. "Glad he don't talk me down."

"Lem?" Sandy replied. "Never! He told me about the time he shot a grizzer off'a you up in the Rockies, and the time you saved his hide durin' the war, and well, I guess you know the rest. I mean, you were there and all."

Slocum smiled and shook his head slowly. "Yeah, reckon I was, reckon I was. But we come to talk to you 'bout somethin' else today. See, we're lookin' for—"

"Rupert Grimes," interrupted Jack. "We got a picture of him. He's a wanted man!"

Slocum shook his head, and pulled out the poster, saying, "Lem and Martha tell me it's not the best drawing, but they thought you hired a man that sort'a looks like him."

Sandy studied the poster. "Well, shit. Sure looks like him. Kinda, I mean. But they caught the eyes, all right. His name—the one he's usin' here, I mean—is Red Garvy. The boys'll be coming in off the range in about three hours. Care to come in and pull up a chair, have some coffee?"

"That'd be swell, Sandy," said Lem. "Slocum, you ain't in no rush, are you?"

"Not me." Then he looked over at Jack. "Somebody might be in more of a hurry," he said, "but he'll calm the hell down for a few hours."

Jack looked at the ground.

"Well, tie your horses to the rail and come on in, then! I just put on a pot'a coffee, and I think we still got some pie left from last night. You like pumpkin?"

Lem nodded happily. "Louise makes the best pumpkin pie you boys've ever set a tooth to. You're in for a real treat!"

"Better than Martha?" Slocum asked, his eyebrows raised in a kidding sort of way.

"Mother don't make no pumpkin pies. Says she was absent the day they taught that."

All the men laughed, even Jack, and then they hitched their horses to the rail, climbed up to the porch, and followed Sandy into the house.

Louise Slade did indeed make one helluva pumpkin pie. She had plenty of leftovers, so Slocum and Jack each had two pieces, complete with freshly whipped cream!

Afterward, the men had a rare afternoon brandy, and they lay the facts before Sandy. "Now, Jack's in trainin', remember? He's got to take this one all by himself, if it's the right feller," Slocum concluded. "Nobody goes to help him, 'less he's in mortal danger. But I don't figure this fella, Rupert Grimes, is gonna put up much of a fight. Whatcha think, Sandy?"

Sandy nodded. "Seems to me like a real peace lover. Ain't drawn his gun since he's been here anyways."

"There you go, Jack. He's all yours."

Jack nodded, although a little shakily. "All mine. Got you."

Lem spoke. "If you get him and he's the one, put a bullet right twixt his eyes!"

Slocum shook his head. "There'll be none'a that, Lem. For starters, the bounty is only if we bring him in alive. If Jack here kills him, then it's his face on a wanted poster next time. And we're not lookin' for that."

Lem grumbled, "Well, you can smack him around a little, can't you? For me? For all the trouble his like has put us through?"

Jack said, "Well, maybe a little," then looked at Slocum as if asking permission.

Slocum looked right back at him and said, "No."

Lem said, "You boys just ain't no fun! I mean, he might be the very same slicker what tried to sell my little spread out from under me!"

Slocum shook his head. "I doubt it, Lem. Those guys are a dime a dozen. 'Sides, the poster says he ain't done that for a while. Lately, he's switched over to rustlin' on a small scale. Now Sandy, I reckon that's why he's here. Wouldn't do for him to take on a big outfit like the Aztec up around

Flag, and Lem's spread is too little. You're middle-sized. Reckon he figured he could take quite a few over a period of time afore you noticed."

Sandy shook his head, his hands balled into fists. "That stinkin' little bastard!"

"I agree," said Slocum, nodding. "But we're not gonna kill him and we're not gonna rough him up. We're gonna take him back down to Phoenix and turn him in, let the law deal with him."

Both Lem and Sandy sat there like two peas in a pod, shaking their heads and looking generally disgruntled. Jack looked scared, but determined. Again, Slocum silently prayed for a simple flesh wound for Jack, then helped himself to a second brandy. He hoped God was listening today. Or that if he was busy, Jesus was standing in for him. Slocum would settle for Buddha or Allah or even Confucius, so long as he could just arrange a little wound for Jack. Nothing serious, nothing life-threatening, just enough to help turn him away from wanting to bounty hunt for a living, and choose a safer occupation.

Slocum glanced at the clock, which now read four thirty-two. He noticed that Jack was staring at it, mesmerized by the rhythmic sway of the pendulum. Four thirty-two, no, thirty-three now. Sandy said he expected the boys back in around five: supper time. Louise was already banging pots around in the kitchen. He guessed that they didn't have a ranch cook, and it all fell on her.

Four thirty-five now. He supposed the hands could ride in at any moment. Most cowhands were an easygoing lot, and could be counted on to do absolutely nothing "on time"— except show up for supper. He expected them sooner than later.

Sure enough, at about a quarter to five, they began to file in. All were freshly scrubbed, courtesy of the horse trough, and some still had beads of water glistening on their ears or necks. As the crew dribbled in, Sandy made the introductions to several of the men, always finishing up with, "And y'all know Lem."

They seemed a friendly bunch. They joked around before they took their seats at the long table between the kitchen and the living room, but once they sat down, they hushed themselves. Slocum thought it must be either out of respect for Louise, or for the coming food, then decided it was more likely both.

As the table gradually filled with bodies, Rupert Grimes was still nowhere to be seen. Jack hissed, "What's keepin' him?" at Slocum.

Who replied, "Shut up. He'll be here when he gets here."

And speak of the devil! Slocum had barely finished his sentence when the front door opened and Rupert walked in, talking with a couple other hands. Sandy stood up, and Slocum and Jack followed suit. Sandy said, "Well, there's the last of 'em." He caught Slocum's eye and winked. "Louise, we're a full crew now."

Louise was already ladling out plates full of beef stew, and the serving plate of biscuits was moving fast around the table. A big bowl of mashed potatoes was swiftly moving in the other direction, followed by a large bowl of steaming green beans.

Sandy had taken his seat at the head of the table by then, but all the other chairs were taken up by the workers. Sandy asked, "You boys don't mind takin' second shift, do you?"

Slocum and Jack shook their heads. Slocum figured that a man with Jack's appetite probably minded, and minded quite a bit, but he kept his peace. For a second there, Slocum was kind of proud. But then he realized what he was proud *of*, and mentally smacked himself.

15

When the cowhands began pushing back from the table and loosening their belts, Slocum decided it was time to take action. He shot a glance over to Jack, who stood up somewhat reluctantly. "Now?" he whispered to Slocum.

"Good a time as any," Slocum whispered back. The buzz of conversation from the table negated their reasons for whispering, but they did it anyway. "Go ahead."

Jack slowly made his way to the table, then around to its other side, stopping once he got behind Rupert. Amid the chatter, he was barely noticed. But he slid his gun from its holster and slowly raised it, so that the muzzle was against Rupert's temple.

"Rupert Grimes, you're wanted for larceny by the Territory of Arizona, and I'm takin' you in," he announced. Rupert went white.

Suddenly, the room was so quiet you could've heard a mouse fart, Slocum thought.

Sandy stood up and addressed the men. "Calm down,

boys. It's true, what Jack here just said. Him an' Slocum rode up from Phoenix, lookin' for him. And they're gonna haul him back down tomorrow. Anybody got a problem with that?"

There was no comment from the table. Slocum noticed the men had moved away from Grimes a little. Although he didn't know how Rupert got along with the other boys, it was always a shock to find out that your saddle pal was a wanted man.

"All right," said Sandy. "If you boys are finished, you can git on down to the bunkhouse. Somebody gather up Grimes's stuff and bring it back up, okay?"

"I'll do it," said a short man farther down the table.

"Good. Now go on, men. Don't say I never provided entertainment with your supper."

A few of the men chuckled into their hands or fists as they filed out, much more sedately than they had filed in. Which left Rupert Grimes at the table, with Jack still holding a gun to his head.

"Jack?" Slocum said.

"Yeah?"

"I think you can put your gun away now."

"Huh? Oh, yeah." He holstered the gun, but not before he had Grimes stand up and relieved him of his guns and gun belt, and made him turn out his pockets. The latter action revealed a pocket knife, but nothing else of interest. He looked toward Slocum again. "What now?"

Christ Almighty! Slocum thought. Had this guy learned nothing? He began to suspect that Jack had a brain like a sieve, holding information for only a day or two, then letting it leak away. Hell, he wouldn't even make a decent shop owner!

Jack gave up on Slocum, who was shaking his head in

disgust, and turned toward Sandy. "Do you have a short length'a rope? Even a lady's scarf'll do."

All right. Maybe he retained a few things. He'd remembered the scarf anyway.

Sandy said, "Got somethin' better. Hang on." And then he went out the front door and closed it behind him.

Jack asked, "What's he gettin', you reckon?"

Slocum shrugged, but Lem smiled and said, "I think I know." But that was all Jack could get out of him.

A few minutes later, Sandy came back in and plopped a pair of iron handcuffs on the table. "There ya go, Jack. Here's the key." He flipped it down on the table, too, and grinned wide.

"Where the hell'd you come by those?" Slocum asked. "I ain't seen any like that since the war."

"That's where they came from. Same's that Gatling gun out front. Same's a few other things I got lyin' around. Self-protection, that's my middle name." He plopped back into his chair and propped his boots up on the table, still smiling with satisfaction. "You boys ever wanna start a war—or end one—you just come see ol' Sandy!"

Slocum chuckled, and Lem laughed out loud. "There he is, folks," Lem managed between bouts of laughter. "My neighbor, the War Lord!"

Sandy smiled before turning toward Slocum. "You boys're welcome to spend the night iff'n you want. I sure wouldn't care to be goin' through Russian Chimes in the dark."

Slocum appreciated Sandy's offer, but declined.

After much back-thumping and *thankee kindly*'s, Lem, Slocum, and Jack set off, with Grimes on foot. His handcuffs were tied by a length of rope to Jack's saddle horn, and he still hadn't said a word. This bothered Jack, but

Slocum said, "Don't worry. He'll talk when he's ready."

By this time they had reached the town of Russian Chimes, and Slocum had to admit—if only to himself—that it was indeed a spooky experience.

The wind had come up some. It mourned and howled through the ramshackle ruins of the buildings, and picked up and carried detritus across the road, slamming it into the men and horses. Advertising signs, long unread, banged against the sides of the peeling, disued buildings that held them as the night darkened and the clouds rolled in, covering the moon.

Fortunately, Lem knew this town and the surrounding countryside like the back of his hand, and led them forward.

When they had left Russian Chimes behind—enough that they were free of its spell anyway—Lem spoke. "I believe she's gonna rain."

Slocum nodded. "I believe you're right, Lem. No thunder or lightning yet, but those clouds sure do look a portent." He glanced over at Jack and was surprised at what he saw. Jack was white as a sheet of new writing paper, likely the result of going through the ghost town. But worse than that, one of his hands gripped the reins and the saddle horn at the same time, and the other was hanging on to Rupert Grimes's handcuff tether for dear life.

Rupert was just trouping along, trying to keep up with the horses.

If Jack could just see himself now, Slocum thought, he'd give up bounty hunting at the first breath of suggestion.

But Slocum couldn't see himself doing any more suggesting so far as Jack's future was concerned. Maybe a little skull bashing, but no more hints or pleas. Jack had to figure this out for himself.

*   *   *

When they rode back down into Lem's ranch, Martha was waiting, and so was supper. Which was fortunate, because the men had forgotten to eat before they rode back from Sandy's ranch. And Martha did herself proud. She had roast beef cooked with onions and potatoes and carrots, biscuits with honey, piping hot coffee, and for dessert, strawberry-rhubarb pie. They let the still-silent prisoner eat with them, and everyone was more than satisfied.

After supper, they took Grimes to the outhouse, then bedded him down in the stable, with the horses. His feet were tied together, then roped to a corner post. His hands, back in the handcuffs, were tethered to the opposite post.

All in all, he was pretty much strung out like a hog ready to be butchered and dressed.

They threw a blanket over him and folded up a smaller one for his pillow, then left him alone, with just the livestock and a dimly turned down lantern for company. Through sheeting rain, they ran back up to the ranch house and Lem's promise of after-dinner brandy and cigars. Slocum would have liked to get another piece of the pie, too. Martha was a wizard of a baker!

Once they'd had their brandy and their cigars, and Slocum had eaten another piece of that good, sugary pie, they started back down to the barn again. The rain had quieted down to a soft, steady patter and the clouds had mostly moved on to the east, so they didn't have to feel their way at least.

The barn, once they got inside, was warm and welcoming. Slocum walked over to Grimes's stall, or at least the one where he was tied down, and asked if he needed to go to the outhouse again. Grimes shook his head no.

In the aisle, Slocum leaned against the stall's outside wall. "You sure don't say much, do you?"

"Somebody once told me it was better to listen than to talk."

Surprised at Grimes's first sentence, Slocum said, "Sounds like a wise man. You're not gonna have to walk to Phoenix, in case you were worried. Lem's gonna lend you a mount."

Grimes snorted. "Wild? Just off the range?"

"I'll see he gets you a decent horse."

There was a pause, then Grimes said, "Thanks. I'd appreciate it," then turned his head away.

Slocum cocked a brow, but that was all.

Slocum turned toward Jack's mare, a couple of stalls down the row. Lem and Jack had set her up nice, in a box stall with deep straw, plenty of hay, and her own water bucket. Still, she was flagging her tail at anything that moved, Slocum included.

He only wished that females of the human sort were that easy. Or that eager.

Although she was a nice mare, Slocum hoped that Jack would take up Lem on his offer to trade him the gelding, straight up, for her. The mare was better looking, but the gelding was sure trained better and had softer gaits, and was more suited to Jack's needs. Lem, on the other hand, wanted her for her wild color, said he'd like to breed a little pinto into his stock. If Jack had any sense, he'd . . .

Slocum shook his head. Sense was one thing that Jack seemed to be perpetually short on.

He'd just have to wait and see. If Jack decided against Lem's offer, they were sure gonna have one helluva bumpy ride back down to Phoenix.

Jack came back inside, having been in the outhouse. He shook off the rain like an old dog and said, "I feel a lot better now."

Slocum nodded. "Bet you do. You leave me any Sears?" An old catalog was a handy thing to have in the outhouse.

Jack nodded. "Yup. And watch out on the left side when ya sit down. Splintery."

"Thanks." Slocum stood back from the stall and patted his pockets in preparation for the outhouse visit. Fixings? Yup. Sulphur tips? Yup. Reading material? Yeah, that, too.

He was all fixed up and ready to go.

He took the spare lantern from Jack and said, "I won't be too awful long."

When Slocum came back from the outhouse, he found Rupert Grimes snoring softly in his stall, and Jack already asleep up in the loft. He shook his head and grinned. Dinner must've knocked them both out.

"Must'a knocked me out, too," Slocum muttered beneath his breath. He grabbed his saddlebags, blew out the lantern down on the main floor, then climbed the ladder, up into the loft.

Picking a spot where the hay was thick, he spread out his blanket, then sat down on it. He would've liked to just lie back and nod off, but he still had things to do, and he wasn't Jack, he reminded himself. No slacking for him.

He dragged over his saddlebags and made sure he was fully stocked up on everything, although he had no doubt that Martha would send them off with a fine feast. There he found Katie's potato salad bowl, wrapped carefully in his winter scarf. He checked it. Not one chip or crack!

For half a second he missed his rope for ringing his pallet, but then decided that, hell, there weren't any snakes up here, and he was safe.

At last, he placed one side of his saddlebags—the one without the bowl in it—down where he was going to lay his head, blew out the lantern, lay back, and went to sleep.

16

The next morning, after a monster breakfast of bacon, eggs, thick toast with butter and jam, sliced and fried ham, fresh strawberries, and coffee, Slocum and Jack bade good-bye to Lem and Martha—who also provided them with a parcel, wrapped in brown paper and tied with string, for their lunch—and set off, back the way they'd come.

Rupert Grimes ate and departed with them, but didn't say a word. He had chosen once again not to speak.

It was no skin off Slocum's nose. So long as Grimes remained in their custody, he could be mute as long as he wanted.

Lem had provided a sorrel saddle horse to transport him back down, and Jack had at least agreed to a temporary trade as far as his transportation was concerned. He was still mounted on Lem's nice gelding. Slocum was satisfied with the arrangements at last, for Rocky was going to be out of luck today.

He stroked the stallion's neck and fed him a lemon drop.

"You'll live," he whispered to the horse. "You won't like it, but you'll live."

Rocky only shook his head in reply.

They traveled south, jogging most of the time, and so made decent time compared to a walk. They stopped to have lunch when they were closer to Phoenix than to Lem's, and Jack opened the box with glee. Martha had been busy, all right.

A whole chicken cut into pieces and fried up so golden and perfect, a container of strawberries, already sugared, and what was left of the mashed potatoes from the night before came out of the box, each to Jack's *oohs* and *aahs*, and each to Slocum's approval. He believed he'd volunteer to take Lem's gelding back up to him. Between Martha and Katie, he could learn to settle down.

For about fifteen minutes, he thought, and gave a shake of his head. Women were sure better cooks than men, but steering a plow horse or threshing hay were among the last things he'd want to do. Even for Katie.

Ah, Katie . . .

How he'd missed her! And it was more than just the absence of somebody to hose, it was the woman herself. Damn, he really *liked* that woman!

He took a bite of Martha's chicken drumstick and chewed while he ruminated. He didn't believe he'd ever thought that before, not and really meant it. He liked Katie, of course. He loved all women, but not so much individually.

Sonofabitch! he thought, incredulous. He liked her.

At that moment, there was a blur of motion beside him, and he stuck out a leg. Tripping, Rupert Grimes fell flat out on the ground with a thud and a painful-sounding groan.

"Watch your prisoner, Jack," was all Slocum said before he took another bite of chicken, then disentangled his leg.

Goddamn amateurs, he thought, and took a long drink of coffee.

Beside him, Jack was struggling first to pull Grimes to his feet again, then to get him in the right place and down on his haunches once more. Slocum heard him mutter, "I swear, Rupert Grimes, I think you're more trouble than you're worth."

Atta boy, Rupert. Just keep him thinkin' along them lines, Slocum thought. Maybe, if he was lucky, Rupert would do him the favor of getting Jack good and sick of the bounty hunting trade. It seemed something Slocum was supremely suited for, but Jack? The trade would eat him up and spit him out. He'd be dead, and then what?

Nothing, he thought. *Just a big, fat nothing.*

After they'd finished up Martha's bounty—and Rupert ate somewhat sheepishly—Slocum packed up Martha's mashed potato bowl and put it away next to Katie's potato salad bowl, muttering, "I swan, sometimes I think I'm just a China carrier . . ."

They each took a long piss on the dying fire they'd built to heat the coffee and warm the mashed potatoes, and saddled up again. Slocum rode out ahead, then Jack, then Rupert, his handcuffs once again connected to Jack's saddle horn by a long rope.

They rode at a steady jog, letting the miles pass away behind them, and then Slocum heard Jack shout his name.

Now what? he thought as he swiveled in the saddle.

He looked at Jack. And he looked behind him.

Jack was the only one there, and he was reeling in the rope that had tethered Grimes to him. It hadn't been cut, just neatly untied.

Muttering, "Sonofabitch," before he remembered that Rupert was only doing what Slocum had wanted him to do, Slocum wheeled Rocky and rode back.

"I swear, Slocum, I don't know what happened!" Jack looked stricken. "I don't know where he went!"

Slocum scratched the back of his neck and said, "Well, not too far. Lem tells me that sorrel he's riding is half lame. Once he pushes him into a lope, it won't be long before he breaks down."

Jack just stared at him, as if he'd suddenly taken to speaking Greek.

Disgusted, Slocum shook his head. "C'mon. Let's go find him."

So they jogged back the way they'd come until Slocum saw where his trail through the grass left theirs, snaking off to the west. It looked like he'd sat there for a minute, most likely waiting for them to get far enough ahead so that they wouldn't hear him scooting off.

He was smart. Slocum would give him that, all right. He didn't know about Jack, but he hadn't heard a thing out of the ordinary.

They pushed into a lope as they followed Grimes's trail, and Slocum was hoping that the sorrel would break down fairly soon. Or not. This whole deal was driving him crazy as a belfry full of bats. On the one hand, he would hate to lose Grimes, who was a penny-ante criminal at best. It would louse up his so-far spotless record for corralling criminals. But on the other hand, it was going to be Jack's capture and Jack's bounty—if they found Grimes, that was—and Slocum didn't want Jack to succeed.

No, that wasn't right. He wanted him to succeed. He just didn't want him to succeed as a bounty hunter, damn it!

After a long afternoon, during which time Slocum let Jack take the lead—which was inevitably the wrong one, each and every time—he had finally had it. He halted Rocky and signaled to Jack to come back. Just as well. He was leading them to Mexico.

The two men faced each other on horseback. The younger, disappointed and nervous. The older was just plain disgusted.

"Jack, you are one mess as a bounty hunter. You're a mess as a tracker. You want me to go on?"

Jack hung his head. "No," he muttered. "I loused up and I know it. I'm sorry."

He out and out hated the kid, but that "sorry" tugged a little at Slocum's heart, as cold and untuggable as he liked to think it was, and he surprised himself by saying, "Well, hell. Let's go find Lem's gelding anyway. Grimes is bound to've cut that horse loose by now."

With Slocum leading the way this time, they backtracked to the place where Grimes had originally separated from them, and set off at a lope. Slocum's practiced eye kept them on course, and eventually, they found where Grimes's tracks indicated his horse was in trouble. It was the old lameness, showing up again.

Jack didn't see it and Grimes probably hadn't felt it yet, but Slocum's practiced eye saw the slight deviation in the track left by the right rear print. He slowed Jack and himself to a walk and kept on for fifteen minutes or so, until their mounts were cooled down and it was too dark to travel much farther. Slocum called a halt to the proceedings.

"Let's camp here," he said when they came to a place where a big old cottonwood stood. Once dismounted, he began to strip the tack off Rocky.

"Hold on," Jack complained. "Can't we go just a little bit farther? You said his horse was breakin' down. He could be smack dab on the other side of this hill, for all we know!"

"Grimes, or the sorrel?"

"Well . . . both!"

"Listen, Jack. Just figure that Grimes is a lost cause.

We're only goin' after the horse now. And I don't imagine he'll wander too far from where Grimes left him." He fastened the hobbles on Rocky's front pasterns. "He's used to bein' taken care of, and livin' in a stable. He won't know what to do out here in the middle'a nowhere."

Jack sighed the sigh of a kid who's just been told he has to go to bed with no dessert, but he started stripping the tack off his gelding.

"Well, what're we gonna do once we find the sorrel?"

"Take him back up to Lem, along with Martha's mashed potato bowl. And try to figure out what you're gonna do for a livin' from here on out."

Surprisingly, Jack looked shocked. "What are you talk' about? I'm gonna be—that is, I *am*—a bounty hunter!"

Slocum had thought this was long settled, and by Jack himself! But he began slowly and said, "Jack, you can't track. You can't hang on to a prisoner to save your life. Look at how you've turned out every damn time you've had to get somebody on your own! If I hadn't been there to save your hide, you'd be dead several times by now."

"But you *are* there!" Jack complained. "I'll learn! I'll get better!"

"No, you won't. At least, I won't be the one to teach you. You either gotta have a knack for this, or you don't. I never thought man-huntin' would come natural to me, but I only been huntin' bounties as long as you, and see the difference? Nope, we've gotta get you into a trade that suits you better."

Jack didn't answer.

Slocum didn't expect him to. He let Jack be, so that he could think things over. He needed to wrap his brain around what Slocum had just said, and to let go of his dreams of being a big-time bounty hunter. Or so Slocum thought.

In the meantime, he gathered enough wood to build a

fire, and the kindling to get it started, and began to slap together some supper. It was lean pickings, made from the stuff in Slocum's saddlebags, but he didn't want Jack to get used to living like the Prince of Persia on the trail. Life was tough out on the open plain. It was time that sank into his head.

After a dinner made up mostly of beef jerky and hot coffee, they lay down under the stars and went to sleep.

Sometime during the night, Slocum was awakened by a soft rustling sound, coming from his left. Slowly, he reached for his Colt and readied it. Might be a puma, he thought, or more likely a bear nosing around for food.

But then he became aware that the "animal" was two-legged, not four, and immediately knew who it was.

"Come on in, Grimes," he said in a low tone. "Suppose you want those handcuffs unlocked."

He flicked his gaze toward Jack, who hadn't roused. It figured.

After three more steps in the darkness, Grimes emerged into the small circle of light emitted by the dying fire. He was armed only with a wooden stick, on the end of which he had somehow managed to make a sort of point.

"You won't need that," Slocum said, digging into his pocket for the key and thinking that if he'd given it to Jack to take care of, he likely would have stuck it in Grimes's back pocket for safekeeping.

Some bounty hunter!

He pulled out the key. "You want me to unlock 'em, or you wanna do it?"

"You," said Grimes, and stepped closer, hands forward, including the one holding the stake. He pointed it at Slocum's heart.

"You don't put that stick thing down, I'm liable to get

nervous and have to use this." Suddenly, his gun was in Grimes's face. Startled, Grimes sucked in air and dropped the stick.

"That's better," Slocum said, and proceeded to unlock the cuffs. He took them from Grimes and slid them into his saddlebags. You never knew when they might come in handy. Then he looked up and asked, "Where's the horse you thieved?"

"Damn thing went lame on me," Grimes responded in a muted tone. He, too, kept glancing at Jack, who was still sleeping soundly. "Turned him loose on the other side'a the hill, over there." He pointed to the northwest.

"All right. Now, get outta here, and don't let me see your face again, got that?"

Looking vastly relieved, Grimes nodded once, then slipped away into the darkness. Slocum listened as his footsteps diminished into nothing.

"Good luck," he muttered to no one in particular, as he prepared to roll a quirlie. "It's a big, nasty world out there, what with all those would-be bounty hunters runnin' around."

Jack rolled onto his side, but he didn't wake.

17

Come morning, Jack woke to find that Slocum had already lit a fresh fire and was brewing coffee. Additionally, Slocum was brushing down the horses—who were munching on a pile of long, fresh grass—and whistling! How could he be so damned chipper when they had ridden all the way up here for nothing?

He struggled up into a sit, and grabbed an empty coffee cup. He was about to pour out a cupful when Slocum shouted, "Give it another five minutes or so, Jack. Just put 'er on," then went back to currying Jack's gelding.

Jack set the pot back, unpoured. Then he sat back, puzzled. What the hell was going on? He had fully expected to wake to Slocum's jabbering at him about giving up bounty hunting, something he had no intention of doing. Slocum was crazy! Had he looked at Jack's bank balance lately, or for that matter, his own?

Bounty hunting was making him rich, making them both rich! Why, a farmer could break his back for a good twenty years and not clear as much as he'd made in the past few weeks!

He'd let one lousy prisoner escape. So what? Everybody had bad days, and he guessed he'd been having one of his. But he'd apologized to Slocum, hadn't he? Not that it was any skin off Slocum's nose anyhow. *It was supposed to be my capture, my bounty!* he thought, equally angry with himself—for losing Grimes—and Slocum—for riding him so hard about it—and Rupert Grimes himself, for getting away in the first place.

And now he was supposed to settle down and do what? Keep a store? Herd cattle? Wait tables?

He didn't think so. He'd done all three for other people, and he couldn't say he'd liked it, liked any of them. Course, if he'd been the owner, like Sam Tompkins up in Flagstaff, then *he* could do the hiring and firing . . . No, he still wouldn't like running a café.

He liked bounty hunting. He liked the changing scenery and the fat bank account. He also liked traveling. Bounty hunting was made for him!

While Jack and the coffee slowly came to a boil, Slocum spent his time between brush strokes staring at the crest of the hilltop to the northwest of them. He was hoping that Lem's sorrel would just sort of wander up and over the hill and save them the trouble of rounding him up. Of course, they'd lose time today. He didn't want to push the lame horse. But they were close enough to Lem's that he could almost spit there, and he'd be damned if they didn't make it by dark.

There was no sign of the horse, though, so when he finished currying and brushing Rocky, he tacked him up and, telling Jack to wait there, rode up the hill. On the other side, past the crest, about a dozen cattle grazed peacefully in the knee-high grass between clumps of cactus. And among them, still wearing his saddle and bridle, grazed Lem's sorrel gelding.

Slocum grinned and shook his head. "I'll be jiggered," he said, and laughed. Some of the cows took a step away at the sound, but the sorrel just kept grazing.

Slocum slowly rode down to him, parting the cattle with as little ruckus as possible. The sorrel simply stood there swishing his tail, even when Slocum bent to catch his reins. "Good boy," he said softly. "That's a good ol' son. Let's get you back to Lem, then."

When he led the sorrel back over the hill, Jack stood up and stared at them. In fact, he stood there, as straight and stiff as if he were at attention, until Slocum had ridden all the way back down to camp and dismounted Rocky. In fact, it wasn't until Slocum's feet hit the ground that Jack's tantrum began.

"Where'd you find him?" he shouted, and all the horses jumped. "How'd you know where he was? Goddamnit, this was all a trick! You had the whole thing laid out afore we left Lem's, you sonofabitch, 'cause you wanted me to lose him, you wanted me to louse it up or think I had, 'cause you wanted to get shed'a me! What're you gonna do? Leave me up at Lem's and then come down and collect Grimes? Have the reward for yourself?"

During Jack's tirade, Slocum's face had become darker and darker, and his hands had balled into fists. He snarled, "Shut the bloody hell up, you worthless little shit!"

And Jack, startled, complied, although he looked like he'd still try to take on a bag full of angry badgers. *He'd lose,* Slocum thought. *And if they didn't finish him off, I would!* He was good and pissed at Jack, pissed enough that if Jack had pushed it, Slocum would have decked him without a second thought.

But Jack did have something going for him: he was basically smart. And some of the time—when he was actually thinking, that was—he used his brain the right way. Which he did at that moment.

He sat back down, folded his hands in his lap, and said, "Sorry."

He didn't look up, not even when Slocum got himself a cup of coffee and a hunk of beef jerky.

"Sorry I called you worthless," Slocum said after he'd chewed some jerky. It was more recanting than he'd ever done, or was likely to do again.

"You were right," Jack said after a moment. He was still looking down at the ground. "Don't say you're sorry 'bout it."

Surprised and puzzled, Slocum stared at him. To begin with, he was shocked at the apology. But he was also wondering whether Jack meant it or not. Three or four hours—or days—from now, was he going to change his mind and set off, hunting outlaws who would surely kill him?

He shook his head. Jack was likely to do just that. But he couldn't control what Jack did, nor did he have a right to. They weren't kin. In fact, they'd barely known each other three weeks. All he could do, to aid in his own self-preservation and that of Jack, was to do his best to discourage the boy—no, he reminded himself, it's *Jack,* not "the boy"—and then get out of town—and shed of him—fast. Slocum figured he might do pretty well up in Colorado. He wasn't wanted there. Well, not very much anyway.

So far as he was concerned, the rest of the mess with Jack was up to the Lord.

Late that afternoon, just before the sun dipped down below the horizon, Slocum and Jack rode into Lem's place, leading his limping gelding behind them. Slocum had checked him out and determined that he'd be all right if they kept it down to a walk, which they had, and they were all tired.

Lem came out of the house just as they rode up, and said, "By God, you fellers is quick! Thought you'd just be gettin' down to Phoenix by now. And come to think of it, I never did fancy the name'a the place. They oughta have left it be Pumpkin Flats. That damn Lord Duppa-Dickhead! He comes around an' tries to change the name'a my ranch, he's gonna have a fight on his hands!"

Slocum broke it, "Lem? We ain't been to Phoenix yet." If he let Lem go on, he could rail for hours about Lord Darryl Duppa—the "dickhead" in question—and his so-called adventures since he hit the Arizona Territory after being paid to leave England by his family.

"What?! Why not? And where's your pris'ner?" Lem peered under the sorrel, as if he might be hiding there.

Jack wasn't saying anything, so Slocum answered. "Lost him at about the halfway point."

"Lost him? *Lost him?*" Lem's face was swiftly turning red. "How the hell couldya do that? You had 'im in chains, fer Christsake!"

Slocum shrugged, and shot a glance over at Jack, who was still staring at the ground. He hated like hell to do it, but he finally said, "All right, Jack. Man up."

Amid a sudden flurry of tears, Jack admitted what had happened, then added, "And Slocum thinks I ought'a be in another business entire, and I don't know what to do!"

By this time, Martha had come out of the ranch house and put her arm around Jack. Casting the words "You two are horrible!" over her shoulder, she walked Jack into the house, all comfort and cuddles. "Come along, Jack, come along and have some pie . . ." Slocum heard her say.

Both he and Lem stood there for the longest time before Lem said, "Well, let's get the horses took care of."

* * *

Inside, Martha had sat Jack down at the table, and pushed a piece of freshly baked apple pie in front of him. It was deep dish, the kind his mama used to make, and his mouth immediately began to water.

But he said, "No thanks, ma'am," and pillowed his head in his hands. He had cried. Cried in front of Slocum, cried in front of strangers. He wanted to die. He wished that Slocum had killed him back down the mountains, when they found Lem's sorrel.

The trouble and embarrassment it would have saved him!

He was so sorry, so sorry about everything: losing his prisoner, yelling at Slocum and calling him names, and now breaking down in front of Lem's place. Slocum was right about him. He couldn't track, couldn't keep his hands on his prisoner, couldn't break up a bar fight, couldn't do anything.

Martha sat down beside him. "Jack, honey? It does a man good to let loose a few tears every now and then. I know you boys, how you're all bravado, but inside, you're just human beings like everybody else. So here."

She handed him a towel. "Scrub your face and blow your nose and eat some'a my dried apple pie, or you're gonna have me to contend with."

She shoved back her chair and stood up, arms akimbo. "And you haven't begun to have a bad day till you got *me* mad at you!"

Jack managed a "Yes'm," and began to scrub at his face. He'd bet he was red as a beet. Or as red as his fanny after a good paddling from his pa, he thought, and then blushed even redder. He blew his nose, set the towel aside, and took the first bite of pie.

It was great! Even better than his ma's, and he told Martha so.

"Don't go talkin' bad about your mama," she said, her

back toward him as she worked. "I'm sure she did the best with what she had. All mothers do." She turned to look at him. "Well. You look a sight better than you did. Are you eating?"

"Yes'm," he answered, then dug back into his pie.

18

Jake was calmed down by the time Slocum and Lem got back from the barn. Jack's mare was still there, and still in full standing season. Slocum figured Jack'd be smart to take Lem up on his offer to trade, even up, for the gelding. But then, Slocum wasn't Jack's keeper, was he? Without opening his mouth, he followed Lem into the house.

Not that he'd had much chance to open it. Lem had been talking, nonstop since they'd arrived. Currently, he was going on about a pinto stallion that Sandy had, and which he'd really like to breed Jack's mare to. If she wasn't Jack's mare anymore, that was.

Martha was setting the table when they got inside, and Jack was at the table polishing off what looked like it had been a bowl of pie. No sign of his tears now. Good. Jack had to learn to man up, goddamn it, and not go around embarrassing people by crying like a girl.

Martha looked up and smiled. "Well, just in time for dinner! And why am I surprised?"

Slocum chuckled and Lem grinned. Jack just kept eating pie.

"We've got roast beef in slices or stew for the hands, and fried chicken for us poor owners and their friends," she went on. "Beans, biscuits and honey, and dried apple pie for everybody. Menu to your satisfaction?" She walked around the table and gave Lem a little peck on his hairy cheek.

"Sounds gut-rattlin' good!" he said, smiling wide enough to expose his gold eye tooth.

"Yes, ma'am, sure does!" said Slocum.

Although he was busy chewing, Jack looked up from his pie and nodded. Nodded happily, Slocum noted. He wondered what kind of magic joy juice Martha put in that pie anyhow.

She turned her attention toward the table. "Hurry along, Jack. You're about to be overrun by a passel of hungry ranch hands."

Jack shoved the last of the pie into his mouth, picked up his bowl and fork, and got to his feet, all in one clumsy move, then carried his dirty dishes to the kitchen. Just in time, too—the hands began to file in, laughing and pushing and shoving. As before, they all took their hats off—and put their manners on—before they sat at Martha's table.

Jack came and joined Lem and Slocum in the living area and rolled himself a quirlie. Lem already had his pipe going and Slocum was halfway through his smoke before Jack had his lit, but he seemed in no hurry. Didn't seem the least little bit upset either, to Slocum's mind. Deciding to leave well enough alone, he simply carried on his conversation with Lem.

"So I said," Lem went on, "why the hell you got all them *steers,* then? I thought you said as how you wanted to raise breeding stock! And ol' Win looks at me and says as how them steers didn't quite measure up to what he wanted, and how he was gonna wait for the next crop to come along. Can you figger that? I mean, why would the next crop be any different? They got the same daddy, they got the same mamas. I jus' figger ol' Win is crazy, y'know?"

Slocum nodded and tried not to appear indifferent, which was what he was. Frankly, he didn't give a flying rat's ass about ol' Win—whoever he was—and his cattle. He was more interested in why Jack was suddenly in such better spirits. No matter how good that apple pie had been, it couldn't have been that good!

And it didn't look to him as if Jack was paying any mind to what he or Lem was saying. His attention seemed to be on the dinner conversation at the table, although why he'd want to listen in was anybody's guess.

"Slocum?" It was Lem.

"Sorry. Just sorta drifted off in my own head there for a minute, Lem."

Lem waved a hand. "Hell, don't be sorry. I do it all the time. Just ask Martha. She's always harpin' on me for wool-gatherin' or daydreamin' or such. So, what'd you think?"

Slocum was at a loss. He said, "Sorry? About what?"

Lem began to laugh like crazy, managing between guffaws to say, "Guess you really was off in the south forty!"

Later, when the hands had gone and Lem, Martha, Slocum, and Jack were just about finishing up their fried chicken, a frantic knock came at the door.

Saying, "I wonder who the hell can that be this late," Lem stood up and went to answer it.

Their visitor was a man Slocum didn't recognize, but who Lem seemed to know, for he asked him in. The fellow was talking gibberish at lightning speed, and Lem held up his hands and said, "Take it easy, Homer, slow down."

Homer, a middle-sized, middle-aged fellow with grizzled red hair, put his hand on his chest and took several deep breaths to calm his ragged breathing.

"That's it, Homer," said Lem. "Remember your heart."

Lem got him set down at the table while Martha ran to get him a drink of water, which he gulped down. "Th-Thank you, ma'am. Beholden to you."

Martha was concerned, but smiled and went to fetch him another glass.

"All right, Homer," said Lem. "What's all the excitement for?"

"Horse thievin'," Homer said.

"No!" Lem said in disbelief. "We ain't had no hoss thieves up here in a coon's age!"

"We do now. Mr. McMurtry's good bay stallion, too! Took 'im right outta the corral, along with a rig'a tack and his good Henry rifle!" Homer was handed his second glass of water and gulped that down as well. "He sent us all out to ride to the nearest ranches, see if they had any trouble."

Lem shook his head. "Nobody's been thievin' around here that I know of." But he shot Slocum a glance that said he was thinking what Slocum was: Rupert Grimes had found himself a mount.

Slocum had explained the whole of the incident to Lem while they were out in the barn, and made Lem promise not to say anything in front of Jack, which he hadn't. It didn't appear that he was going to now either, thank God. He didn't need Jack to all of a sudden go chasing after somebody who was likely halfway to the California border by now.

But Jack's ears had perked up anyway, dammit. He had leaned forward and was staring at Homer. "Any idea what time they took him?" he asked.

Homer said, "Can't put it in a box or anything, but sometime betwixt nine o'clock last night and six this morning.

Nine's when our last rider comes in from checkin' the border, and six is when we all get up."

Jack nodded. "Thanks."

"Don't go gettin' any ideas," Slocum growled, low and in Jack's direction.

But Homer was watching. "You fellers got an idea who might'a took him?"

Slocum was hoping that Jack would be too embarrassed to say he'd lost a prisoner who could be suspect in the theft, but he was wrong.

Jack said, "I got an idea, a good idea. Feller called Rupert Grimes. He was afoot the last we heard of him, right, Slocum?"

Slocum slouched back. This guy was trying to kill himself as fast as he could, and Slocum wasn't going to be a part of it. He said, "That's true. But Jack lost him once already, and I ain't gonna go through that again."

"Slocum!" said both Jack and Lem in unison. Jack looked shocked—and ashamed—and Lem simply appeared surprised.

"Just what the heck *are* you two boys? U.S. marshals?" Homer asked.

"Hardly," said Slocum. "I'm a bounty hunter, and we're not exactly sure what Jack is yet."

Lem nodded. "True, Slocum, true. You best stay outta this, boy."

But Jack said, "I will not! And you two stop gangin' up on me!" He stood straight up. "I'm goin' after him, and I'm goin' right now!"

"Sit the hell down," barked Slocum, and Jack unconsciously obeyed, although with a scowl on his face. "First off, it's dark out. How you gonna track him at night when you can't track him in the blarin' sunlight?"

Jack had no answer, except for the dirty look he shot Slocum's way.

Slocum ignored it and carried on. "Second, he's ridin' a faster, more powerful horse than you got. And third, now he's got horse thievin' to add to that poster. It's gonna make him worth more money, but it's also gonna make him more dangerous to catch. He won't have a second thought about pluggin' you in the back."

Jack sat there, scowling, head down. Then he suddenly looked up and said, "Homer, I'm startin' out after Rupert Grimes first thing in the mornin'. And don't try to talk me out of it, Slocum. I'm gonna prove myself to you and ever'body else!"

"Even if it kills you?" Lem asked.

Slocum just rolled a quirlie and lit it. If this kid was anything, it was headstrong. He'd tried to change his mind, tried every way he knew how, but Jack's mind was set. There was no turning back now.

"Really?" asked Homer, half disbelieving. "You'll really go after him?"

Jack gave a curt nod. "First thing in the morning."

"Hot damn! Mr. McMurtry's gonna be real pleased!"

Slocum blew out a cloud of smoke and, under his breath, muttered, "For a little while anyway."

Slocum actively avoided Jack—and Jack's questions—for the rest of the evening, and when he rose, blinking, at dawn, Jack wasn't there. He hadn't taken his mare either. He'd taken the gelding he'd borrowed from Lem.

Slocum was in a quandary. He couldn't decide whether to go after Jack and at least retrieve Lem's gelding, or whether he should simply write Jack off. The horse would probably come home on its own, once Grimes or somebody else shot Jack off him.

And then, too, Grimes would be wanted for both horse

theft and murder in addition to his other crimes, which would really push the reward up . . .

No. Not Jack.

Slocum mentally slapped himself, then climbed down the hayloft ladder to the ground level of the barn. He didn't know why he cared so much about some green kid. But he'd been a green kid once himself. But he'd got the green scrubbed off him pretty damned fast, compared to Jack.

"I think he's just dead set on ending up, well, dead," he said to Lem on the front porch, while they waited for the hands to finish so they could grab some breakfast.

"Seems to me you're right," Lem admitted. "I once knew a feller like that, back in El Paso, in Texas. He wanted to live by the gun. Ended up dyin' by it." He shrugged. "What goes around comes around, I reckon."

Although he wasn't one to ask for other people's opinions, Slocum thought highly of Lem, and therefore said, "You figure I should go after 'im?"

"Well, you're a lot less likely to get yourself killed, that's for sure. Maybe you'll get lucky and find him wanderin' around out there, not knowin' where he is or which way's up."

"That's what I'm hopin'," said the big man. He had just about decided that he'd better go after Jack, dammit, and take his chances. But he wasn't going into California, no sir! There was far too much paper out on him over there, and far too many people who'd recognize him.

The screen door opened. To the background sound of scraping chairs, Martha stood in the doorway, a smile on her face and a dish towel over one arm. "You boys want to grab some breakfast, now's your chance."

Slocum stood and held out her mashed potato bowl. "Sorry, ma'am. Forgot I had it. That dinner you fixed for us was sure good!"

19

Slocum set out toward McMurtry's ranch, after getting directions from Lem. Breakfast had been good, but it wasn't
setting well with him. That damned Jack! When he found
him, he was going to wring his bloody little neck! No, he
wasn't. A visit to the back house was what he needed, a
good old-fashioned whipping.

He mulled over just what, exactly, was the best punish-
ment for Jack, until he realized that whatever discipline
Jack deserved, he was going to get—either at the hands of
Rupert Grimes, or from the Universe, by way of being ter-
minally embarrassed by ending up lost.

Again.

He found McMurtry's place with no problem, and noted
from the sign out by the gate that it was the Double M. He
rode on up to the house, and a man stepped out to greet
him. Well, "greet," he supposed, was being generous. The
middle-aged man—older than he, but some younger than

Lem—was holding a shotgun with both barrels cocked, and it was pointed straight at him.

"McMurtry?" he asked.

"That's the name. What you want it for?"

He braced his hands on the saddle horn. "My name's Slocum. I understand that you had a horse stole last night."

McMurtry's neck turned red under the grizzle of his beard. "So what?"

"So, I aim to try and get him back for you. My partner, Jack, rode over earlier this mornin'. Wondered, could you tell me which way he took off?"

"Oh," said McMurtry, and lowered the barrel of his shotgun, at the same time gently thumbing down both hammers. "He was here, all right. Couple'a my boys rode with him. They took off thataway." He pointed toward the southwest.

Slocum sniffed. "Headed for California, I imagine. Wantin' to avoid the Bradshaws."

"That's what I figured."

Slocum touched the brim of his hat. "Reckon I'll be off, then. Thanks."

McMurtry nodded curtly. "Best'a luck to you."

"Gonna need it," Slocum muttered as he turned Rocky around and headed back out the gate. Grimes was doing just what he'd figured he would, and Slocum was ready for him. Of course, he didn't know how trail-savvy Grimes was. He could be as green as Jack, for all Slocum knew.

That'd be just great. The blind leading the blind.

He soon found the trail and pushed Rocky into a lope. Well, he didn't exactly need to push him. Rocky was raring to go, and all it took to change his gait was easing up a bit on the reins. Slocum spotted Jack and the two Double M hands about a half hour later. They were up ahead, resting their horses.

As Slocum came loping, then jogging in, Jack stood up, a shit-eating grin on his face. *Here it comes*, Slocum thought.

And he didn't miss the mark. "Glad to see you, glad to see you!" Jack said at his most jovial. He looked like the cat who'd just swallowed the canary. Slocum wanted to punch him square in the beak, but held himself back. He also refrained from dismounting.

He noticed the Double M hands both readying their horses, and asked, "Where they goin'?"

"Back to the ranch, I guess. We lost the trail. But now that you're here—"

Slocum held up his hand. "Whoa. Just hold on. What makes you think I'm gonna help?"

"Because you're Slocum! Because you always do!" Jack whined, to the point that one of the hands turned around and looked at them curiously.

Slocum sighed in resignation. "All right. Get your damned horse."

"Great! And thanks!" He sprinted over to the horses and began readying his gelding.

Both of the Double M men rode off, tipping their hats to Slocum as they passed him.

Grudgingly, he nodded in acknowledgment and, under his breath, muttered, "You boys're gettin' off easy . . ."

Slocum found the trail, and then let Jack follow it. When Jack veered off the trail about fifteen minutes later, clearly— to Slocum's eye anyway—the trail of a lone steer passing through the grass, he didn't say anything. Nor did he say a word when Jack cut off that track to follow some mule deer that had wandered through. Slocum was sorry that they weren't going to bring back McMurtry's stallion, but at least Jack wasn't going to get himself killed. And Slocum would be back in Phoenix all that much sooner, sampling

Katie's cooking along with her other copious charms.

All in all, he thought, the day was going pretty well.

But then Jack suddenly stopped. Slocum rode up next to him and halted, too. He said, "What's the trouble?"

Jack said, "Well, look! I had a good trail to follow, and it's all of a sudden turned into rock!"

Slocum looked ahead. The land before them was, indeed, flat rock for as far as the eye could see, the remains of some ancient volcanic flow. Slocum was familiar with this type of terrain. You could track on it if you were tracking something shod, but it took a very practiced eye and even closer scrutiny.

He didn't tell this to Jack, though. First, you sure couldn't track unshod mule deer over it, and second, what was Jack gonna do with some mule deer anyway?

So he scratched the back of his neck. "Looks like you lost 'im. Sorry." He was getting to be a pretty fine liar of late, he thought, and shook his head.

Jack sat there a moment while his gelding swished flies, then said, "Y'know, back there when the trail split, I thought for sure that this was Grimes. But maybe it wasn't. Maybe he just kept goin' on. Somethin' did anyhow."

Slocum knew he'd lose this one, no matter what, so he said, "All right. Let's backtrack." Once again, he let Jack lead the way.

At least Jack was better at dogging his own trail than he'd proven the day they lost Grimes. They were back where the trail veered off in a couple of hours, and he started down the other trail, after the lone steer, when Slocum said, "Hold up. Time we rested the horses."

"Oh," Jack said rather sheepishly, and added, "Right here? Or you wanna go over by the trees?"

"Trees," Slocum said. At least they'd have someplace to tie the horses instead of hobbling them.

They rode to the stand of cottonwoods, settled the horses, and broke out the hardtack and jerky. Slocum found a little stream nearby, and so they had fresh water to brew a pot of coffee.

"You're gonna make coffee?" Jack asked, his eyebrows arched, when Slocum came, carrying the pot from the stream. "Won't we lose a lotta time that way?"

Slocum just shrugged and began to dig out the Arbuckle's. "Rest. Take a snooze iff'n you want. I won't let you sleep too long."

Puzzled, Jack took himself a hunk of jerky, and sat down, his back against a rock. "I swear, Slocum. I don't understan' you at all sometimes."

Slocum kept his eyes on the coffeepot, which he was placing on a rock at the edge of the fire. He said, "Good. That's part'a my plan. Jus' be glad you get me some'a the time, Jack."

He glanced up just in time to see Jack aim a puzzled expression skyward, then rip into his jerky. Slocum sat back. The coffee wouldn't be ready for at least fifteen or twenty minutes, and he wanted to close his eyes for a second or two. Baby-sitting was hard work.

They set off after the break, following the steer track. Jack still hadn't realized the difference between shod horse hooves and two-toed cattle prints, and Slocum realized he was just following the bent grass, never looking beneath it.

But that was Jack's way, wasn't it? He never scratched the surface of anything, unless he was told to. He was a better follower than he was a leader—that was for sure. Of course, there was nothing wrong with that. Slocum figured not everybody could be a leader, or the world would be total chaos.

But Jack's trouble was that, although he didn't think like

a leader or act like one most of the time, in his mind, he thought he was one.

He was grossly misguided.

But Slocum—who never thought of himself either way, but only as a lone wolf sort of a fellow—intended to work on that situation. He was working on it now. He followed the steer tracks—and Jack—on through the long grass, and he was counting on Jack wasting as much time as possible.

So far, Jack was succeeding at that part, at least.

Not too far away, Rupert Grimes rested himself and his horse. He had tied the stallion to a bush, watered him, and then watered himself. He was good and thirsty. Although he was accustomed to being in the saddle all day, he wasn't used to being chased, and he was certain that either McMurtry's men or Slocum—or both—were after him. And that, in itself, could bring on a powerful thirst.

He knew he wasn't much of a trail hand. If Lem had hired him to drive his cattle back to Kansas City, he'd be halfway to Canada instead. He was bad at tracking, too, and only a fair hand with a gun. With a rifle, he was much better—at least you could look down the sights—but how many shoot-outs were there out here where both men were shooting rifles at each other?

Those were the main reasons he'd taken to mail-order schemes in the first place. You didn't have to go anywhere or do anything other than speak and write English, and have enough legal knowledge to draw up a paper that looked legal to the unpracticed eye, but wasn't.

He'd worked in a law office back home in Baltimore, so he knew a little about drawing up legal papers. At least, he'd copied a few in his time and was familiar with legal language and terms. Also, a little Latin. That came in handy, too. How he'd ended up in Arizona, herding cattle and riding a horse for a living, was a long and convoluted story. But he had six steers stashed in a little box canyon not too far from here— he thought—and he was going to try to get them. At least he'd have a little traveling money.

Hidden in a secret compartment in his saddlebags—which Lem and Slocum had so nicely made certain were strapped to the back of his saddle—he had enough money to buy himself a modest property, a horse, a carriage, and furniture, and live for about a year before he had to seek employment. The cattle money would give him transportation money and a little extra.

Maybe a crystal chandelier.

He grinned, although there was no one there to grin back at him. Life was good, if those fellows would just quit chasing him. He'd send McMurtry's horse back once he got to a town, and then everything would be all right.

He hoped.

Western criminals, except for the hardcore kind, rarely made an impact on the back-East populace. He was fairly sure that nobody would pay any mind to a petty pencil pusher who was last reported around Russian Chimes in the Arizona Territory. Plus, he had decided to grow a beard and mustache. He thought it might make him look worldlier, too, besides being a good disguise.

He stood up, stretched, and went to his horse. Well, McMurtry's horse.

He snugged up the girth again, and the blasted thing tried to kick him. He wouldn't have taken the stallion if it hadn't been the only animal in the corral. Frankly, the damned thing was so vile tempered that it was more trouble than it was worth.

And then he remembered that Slocum rode a stallion, too. That one had seemed nice mannered. Maybe it was a difference between the kinds of horses—the quarter horse he was riding, and the Appaloosa that Slocum was on—that made their temperaments so opposed to one another. Or maybe Slocum was just a better horseman that he was.

He didn't know. And frankly, he didn't much care.

All he knew for certain was that when he got back to Baltimore, he was going to buy a nice, settled gelding to pull his carriage.

20

Slocum caught himself a few winks, had a cup of coffee, then woke up Jack, who came awake, although somewhat groggily. "Coffee?" Slocum asked, but Jack shook his head no.

"Water," he said. "Instead." He shoved a thumb to the west. "Stream down thataway?"

Slocum nodded, and Jack stood up, a little creakily, and made for the water.

"Don't fall in and drown," Slocum muttered once he was out of sight, even though he knew the creek was only eight or ten inches deep. It would be just like Jack to kill himself that way.

But he shook his head. No, things were going great. They had lost Grimes for good, and he was going to get Jack returned to Phoenix with no more aspirations of bounty hunting, and with a good bit of money in the bank.

Maybe, if he didn't want to own anything, business-wise,

he could get hired on as a ranch hand. Maybe even Lem would want to hire him!

No, Lem was a longtime friend. Slocum wouldn't do that to him.

But there had to be something that Jack could do, and do well, that would make him happy. At least, happy enough to forget about bounty hunting.

Jack, looking refreshed, came back over the hill and, once he got to Slocum, said, "You'll never guess."

Slocum just looked at him. Then, "What?"

"This isn't Grimes's track either! It's a steer, a goddamn steer! I saw his prints clear enough where he crossed the creek, and he's grazin' about a hundred yards away on the other side." He sat down with a squishy plop, having managed to get his boots and pants wet, and slumped over. "I'm really no good. No damn good at all."

Slocum let those words hang in the air for a few minutes before he said, "Maybe not, Jack. Just 'cause you're no ace at bounty huntin' don't mean there ain't somethin' out there you're good at. Maybe somethin' where you could be the best!"

Jack looked up. "You really think so?"

"Look. You're a smart kid when you wanna be. So far, you've ruled out bounty huntin'. It ain't exactly the most respectable trade anyhow."

"But it's good enough for you!"

"I ain't the respectable type. For me, it don't matter. But for you, there might be somethin' a whole heap better to do with your time. Hell, you could end up being a U.S. senator or somethin'!"

Jack sat up straight. "A senator," he said softly, and smiled. "Senator Jackson R. Tandy." His smile broadened, then he said, "Maybe I could even be president!"

"You got to aim high, Jack."

Jack breathed, "President Tandy . . ."

"But you got to start low. You gotta figure out where to do it and what to do first. I ain't no political advisor, but there's folks in Phoenix who know about that stuff. Ask 'em. The worst that can happen is they tell you to get lost. So then you go to the next one. Like that."

Jack nodded, his grin unshakably in place.

"Let's mount up and get back to Lem's, then," Slocum said, rising. The rest of the coffee was poured on the fire, putting it out. "You gotta figure out what you're gonna want to do with that mare'a yours."

Jack stood up, too. "Right. You know, Slocum, I think I'm gonna take Lem up on the trade. This gelding's a lot easier to sit at a trot than she is."

Slocum glanced up at the sky, thinking, *Thank You. I reckon there's hope, after all.*

Jack ran out of energy about halfway to McMurtry's ranch, and Slocum took pity on him, suggesting that they rest the horses. Jack took him up on it right off, and they stopped in the precise middle of nowhere, surrounded by knee-high grass and an occasional cactus clump.

"Reckon you can stand this for a short spell?" he asked Rocky as he strapped on the hobbles. The horse snorted in reply and shook his head. "Okay, okay," said Slocum. He slipped the stallion's bridle off, then fed him a lemon drop. "Go eat in comfort."

He had noted Rocky gazing off toward the foothills to the west several times, but paid it little mind. It was probably a mare in season, somewhere in the territory. Old Rocky had a good sniffer when it came to things like that.

Slocum shook his head and grinned.

Jack was already passed out in the grass, and he grinned at that, too. He figured he could afford to at this stage of the game.

He was about to sit down and smoke a quirlie when a shot rang out.

It hadn't hit anything that he could see, but he dove deep into the grasses just in case. What kind of fool was out here hunting on cattle land? And what kind of idiot would fire when he could plainly see there were two hobbled horses out in the open?

Rocky, being accustomed to such goings-on, was already making his way slowly toward a fan of prickly pear about eight feet high. He moved slow, on account of the hobbles, but he was getting there. Slocum whistled. He couldn't remember Jack's horse's name, if he'd ever known it. He called, "C'mon in, c'mon, boy!" But Rocky turned toward him instead.

"No!" he yelled, and motioned away from himself with his hand. "Cactus! Go to the cactus!"

The stallion looked at him quizzically, then resumed his previous direction. Slocum had gotten to his knees while trying to save the horses, and suddenly felt a sharp pain and a good bit of pressure—enough to knock him over backward—in his upper arm. It wasn't until he hit the ground that the sound of the slug being fired came to his ears.

He was thinking that it was good it was the left one that had been hit when Jack suddenly appeared, crawling through the grass toward him, chanting, "Oh, damn, Slocum! Slocum, are you all right? Slocum, say somethin'!"

"What you want me t'say?" Slocum managed.

"You're alive!" Jack practically shouted. "Alive, alive!"

"Shut up!" Slocum snapped as he pulled himself into a sit. "And keep your damn head down."

Jack crouched down a little more.

Slocum said, "It came from out there." He pointed toward the foothills. "'Bout a half mile off, I reckon."

When Jack just stared at him, he added, "From the time between the bullet and the sound. Slugs travel faster."

Before Jack had time to tell him that he wasn't making any sense, he had begun to crawl toward Rocky, and the shelter he had found behind the cactus.

Rupert Grimes, crouched down in the foothills, scowled, and searched the grassy expanse once more. Both men had gone down in the grass, and now the only thing he could see to shoot was the gelding Jack had been riding, and an occasional glimpse of Slocum's stallion's rump.

This had been a bad idea.

He should have just let them go on their way, just stayed the hell out of it. They'd been going away from him, hadn't they? He thought they were going east, but he could be wrong about that. He'd always been bad at directions. For all he knew, he could be up in Utah by now, or maybe Colorado.

Did they have trains in Denver? Of course they did! He could get back to Baltimore from there. If only he could find it . . .

He'd changed his heading more times than he could count. He started out trying for California. He knew he'd have to cross the Colorado River to get there, but he sure hadn't found any river. Not yet anyway. He'd found a couple of little streams, but nothing which, in his wildest imagination, he would've called a river. For the umpteenth time, he wondered if he'd gone far enough.

But Sandy's hands always spoke of it like it was just over the hill, just next door! Two of the boys had ridden to San Diego on an errand for Sandy, and it had taken less than a week. And San Diego was a long way to the south, too, according to them and the old map he'd glanced at.

And just then, something popped up out of the grass. A man! Grimes was a good and careful shot, and he squeezed off one round. The fellow dropped like a stone.

There. He'd done it. He'd never killed anybody before and he was sorry to mess up his record, but on the other hand, who was going to find out? The horses would probably wander back to Lem's, eventually, and who could find anything at all in that long grass? No, he felt secure. And once he sent McMurtry's damned stallion back, nobody would care. Certainly nobody in Baltimore.

Nobody out here either.

He figured he'd taken Slocum out with the second slug, and Jack out with the third. The first one probably hadn't hit anything but cactus. Well, it was rough getting used to a new rifle. He liked McMurtry's Henry, though. It had a good feel to it, and it shot straight. Two important things, when you were considering a firearm.

He stood up and dusted off his knees. Still no movement in the grass out there. Having left McMurtry's stallion tied to a stump back behind some rocks, he set off to retrieve him.

He had just pivoted on his heel when something hit him in the back and knocked him right down on his face. Then came the sound of the bullet.

"What?" he muttered, at just about the time he realized he couldn't move his legs.

Slocum saw him go down, but watched through the rifle's sights a little longer, trying to catch any hint of movement.

There wasn't any.

At last, he lowered the rifle. "Jack!" he called. "Jack? You there?"

Silence was all that greeted his calls. He slid the rifle

back into the saddle's boot, secured it, and then dropped to his knees. He'd lost a lot of blood.

Doing the crawl on one arm and two knees, he started back through the long grass. It didn't take him long to find Jack—sprawled in the grass, and unconscious.

At first, Slocum thought he was dead. It wasn't until he held his Colt's muzzle beneath Jack's nose that he could tell he was breathing. But he'd been gut shot, and that in itself was sure enough a death sentence. It was just a matter of time.

Grimes was in pain, at least from the chest up. He still couldn't move his legs, let alone feel them. Pissed at himself for getting shot, he was also pissed at whoever had done it.

All he wanted was to go home to Baltimore and forget everything about the so-called charms and excitement of the West. He hated the West, hated its hardships, hated its wide-open spaces, its snakes and spiders and broncos and steers and women, which were either tramps or icebergs. And he liked his steak on a plate, cooked medium rare, thank you, and he didn't wish to see it any other way for the rest of his life.

Which was looking pretty damned short, if you asked him. Whoever had shot him had better come to collect him, and pretty soon, he thought. He could still move his arms, and he'd reached around to feel his back. His shirt was sopping with blood. But then, the doctors out here weren't much good. Why did he think they'd be able to fix him, even if he lived to see one?

And what made him think that whoever had shot him wouldn't just ride up here and finish the job once they arrived?

He was in a bad spot, like his Pop used to say. In fact, he couldn't remember ever having been in a worse one.

After giving the matter due consideration—and allowing time for his hopelessness to build from a swell to a tidal wave—he reached down and retrieved his—well, somebody back at the Double M's—handgun.

He cocked it, then pressed its cold barrel to his temple. He whispered, "Mama, Pop, I'm comin' your way. I hope."

He pulled the trigger.

21

Slocum had left Jack in the weeds and was halfway to the shooter's vantage point when he heard the shot. It was a handgun this time, not the rifle he'd been using. For a second, he wondered what had made the guy change weapons, and then he knew. He urged Rocky ahead, leaving the grass behind and traveling over tough volcanic rock, upward and upward, until he came upon the site.

Grimes lay in a pool of blood that had mostly welled from his back, by the looks of it. In his hand was a Colt revolver, which accounted for the hole blown clear through his head.

On the ground, Slocum stood over him and muttered, "Shit," his head shaking slowly.

Leaving Rocky behind, he went to find McMurtry's stallion, and discovered him just around some boulders, tied to an old stump and looking pretty damned spooky. "It's all right, fella," he cooed as he walked slowly up to the stud, while extending a palm holding one of Rocky's lemon drops. "It's all right, boy."

*   *   *

A few moments later, he had Grimes's body, still dripping blood, tied securely over the stallion's back, and had switched the stallion's bridle for a halter, although he'd moved the bridle's curb chain to the halter and tied the lead rope to one end of it. It made him feel like he had a little more control anyway.

Now came the test. He led the stud a few feet toward Rocky, then mounted up. He studied both horses' posture, their ears, and their eyes. So far, no trouble.

McMurtry's bay was still a little jumpy, but Slocum would allow him that. He'd probably never hauled a dead man before. And Rocky? He was his old affable self, and currently crunching the lemon drop Slocum had given him just before he mounted.

"All right, fellers," Slocum said. "Let's go down and get Jack."

They started down the slope, skidding a little on the loose gravel as they went. In the far distance, Slocum could see Jack's gelding still placidly grazing. Damn that horse anyway! You'd think the horse would at least show . . . And then he stopped himself.

Why would the gelding show anything at all where Jack was concerned? Where anyone was concerned, for that matter?

He got a grip on himself. He was wasting time thinking about Jack's horse when he should have been thinking about Jack, lying down there in the grass. Or thinking about his burden and the stud horse next to him. It was a dangerous thing, two studs traveling side by side, but not as dangerous as it could have been—Jack could have traded Lem back for his mare. Slocum figured he could handle Rocky under those circumstances, but McMurtry's stud? He couldn't be counted on for anything, except to be jumpy.

And Jack. He figured to take him back to Lem's. It was a good bit closer than Phoenix, and he wanted to get him into a bed and comfortable—well, as comfortable as a gut-shot man could be anyhow—as soon as possible.

What if Jack couldn't ride? Slocum decided to build him a travois. There was likely enough wood around and he thought that between his coil and Jack's, he'd have enough rope to lash something together. If Jack's horse would pull it.

Well, dammit, if Jack's horse wouldn't, he knew Rocky would.

He slowed the horses down from their jog when he spotted Jack in the grass. He was still where Slocum had left him, but he'd rolled to one side. That was a good thing. He hoped the man was still breathing.

When he got closer, he hopped down and went to Jack.

"Jack? Jack, can you hear me?" he said.

Jack's eyelids fluttered a little, and he croaked, "Slocum? What happened?"

Slocum let out an enormous breath, then said, "It's okay, Jack. You're shot, but you're gonna be fine. Can you sit up?"

With Slocum's help, Jack struggled up into a sit, holding his belly and moaning. Slocum didn't like the sound of it, but said, "I'm gonna try to get you up on your horse, Jack. You think you can help me?"

Jack didn't answer, just nodded in the affirmative.

"Okay, then. You wait here while I fetch your horse, all right?"

Jack nodded again.

Slocum ran for the horse, slipped off his hobbles, and jumped on, riding him back, only to leap off again when he neared his goal.

But Jack was down again. Damn!

Once he got a tourniquet tied around his own upper arm—it wouldn't do Jack any good if he passed out from blood loss—it took Slocum a good half hour to get Jack on his feet and up on his horse, and even then he roped him into his saddle. He was still woozy with the pain, and Slocum found himself thinking that he wished he had some laudanum on him.

Slowly, at a walk, he began leading a slouched-in-the-saddle Jack and a very dead Grimes back up toward Lem and Martha's ranch.

"Jesus Christ, what happened to him?" was the first thing out of Lem's mouth when he saw Jack. He'd been out front when Slocum came riding up.

"Gut shot," Slocum said. He was already down and untying Jack from the saddle. Jack thanked him by falling into his arms, unconscious. "Help me get him inside, Lem."

The two of them carried Jack inside and down the back hall to what Slocum assumed was a spare room. Martha followed them, all aflutter. She said, "Lem, hadn't you ought'a ride for Doc Witherspoon?" once they had him on the bed. "I can take it from here," she added, elbowing Slocum out of the way.

Slocum knew when he wasn't wanted, and retreated back to the front room, followed by Lem. As he strapped on his gun belt, Lem said, "Who's the other feller? The one out there."

"Rupert Grimes."

Lem nodded. "Bet this is a real interestin' story, but I'll get it later." He walked out the front door, Slocum on his heels, and grabbed Jack's borrowed gelding off the rail. "I'll be back with Doc Witherspoon in about an hour, if he ain't in the middle of an emergency or some-such."

And then he galloped off, disappearing into the tree line.

Slocum gathered up the reins and lead rope of the other two horses and set out for the barn. He had to do something. He might as well get them settled in for the night. As it was, it was almost dark. He hoped ol' Lem knew that trail like the back of his hand.

He also hoped that McMurtry'd had the presence of mind to report his stallion missing. To somebody. Slocum wasn't quite sure how far he'd have to ride to get that done, but if there was a doctor within a half-hour's ride, like Lem had said, then it made sense that there was a town, too.

Towns came and went so fast in the territory, it was hard to keep track of them.

In the barn, he stabled McMurtry's stud as far away as possible from Rocky, tying them in their box stalls for good measure. He tied a fresh tourniquet on his arm and tightened it as best he could. Then he curried and brushed both horses and gave them feed, hay, and water.

Satisfied that they were seen to—and that Lem would be back any minute now—he adjourned to the front porch and rolled and lit himself a quirlie. The hands began piling in, looking for a supper that Martha hadn't had time to make, what with tending the wounded Jack. But it appeared that they made do. Slocum heard Martha's voice for a moment, although he couldn't make out the words, and then some commotion in the kitchen.

Later, the hands filed out, all looking well fed. A few stopped to talk to Slocum and express their sympathy about Jack's injury.

He thanked each one, and then warned them about the dead man in the barn. He'd left Grimes's body in one of the stalls.

In turn, they thanked him, then headed off toward either the barn, to settle in their horses if they hadn't yet (or get a look at the corpse), or to the bunkhouse, to turn in or play cards.

Slocum knew what he'd be doing if he was one of them,

but right now he was too focused on the path Lem had followed when he left to think about it. He was already a half-hour past due.

It wasn't until Slocum had smoked three quirlies and was nervously rolling a fourth that he saw Lem coming down the trail, along with another mounted man. The doctor, he presumed.

He was right. After they dismounted, Lem introduced him as Dr. Witherspoon. Witherspoon greeted Slocum somewhat curtly, pulled his bag down off his horse, took one look at Slocum's arm, and said, "Well, you're a mess, too!" and headed on into the house, shouting, "Martha? Martha, it's Doc Witherspoon!"

Over the next few days, Slocum learned quite a few things.

First off, he learned that McMurtry had, indeed, reported the stallion as stolen to the local authorities, and also reported Grimes as the man who'd stolen him. That was good, very good, indeed. It'd jack up the price on Grimes.

He also had a short visit with the local sheriff, to whom he turned over Grimes's body and recounted their last shootout to the south. Nodding, the sheriff said it sure sounded like self-defense to him, and duly hauled the body back to town, which Slocum learned was called Troubadour. It seemed an awfully fancy name for a fly-by-night mining town in the West, but he kept his opinion to himself.

Martha, despite nursing Jack in addition to her regular ranch duties, remained in good spirits, although she was concerned about Jack, as they all were. It appeared that Slocum had been wrong about gut shot being a death sentence. At least, the doc thought so.

He'd told Slocum and Lem that in the past, it had been a sure but lingering death, but that lately, somebody or other had discovered there were things called germs—little tiny things, so tiny you couldn't even see them with the naked eye—that spread through the system and killed you.

Turned out that Doc Witherspoon wasn't one of those fellows who had started out as a barber, but was a real, honest-to-God, trained doctor and a graduate of Harvard University, back East. Lem said he had a diploma on his wall and everything.

This, in itself, was enough to impress Lem, but Slocum was more impressed by the fact that Jack kept improving a little each day. The doc'd had to open him way up to get out the slug, which had bored a hole through his intestines and followed a circuitous route before coming to a halt in his liver. Doc Witherspoon had worked on Jack long and hard, but although he said that gut wounds were no longer always fatal, he also said that Jack had been shot bad, and his chances were about fifty-fifty.

Jack now had a scar he could be proud of—from below his belly button around to the middle of his back. Doc saved the slug and gave it to Martha for safekeeping, in case Jack made it through and wanted a keepsake.

The doc kept close tabs on Jack, coming every afternoon to see him and checking Slocum's arm while he was there.

As for Slocum himself, he got bored on the second day, seeing as how Jack seemed to be getting better, and started riding out with the hands. It felt good to be doing some good, purposeful riding. And it was good to get back to ranch work. He taught Rocky a few things about reining and sliding stops while he was at it, too, as well as calf roping and holding a taut line.

By the fourth day, Jack seemed to turn a corner, but not a corner anybody wanted him to turn. He began to vomit blood and show it in his stool, and every time Slocum checked on him, he was as white as a sheet of paper.

The doc shook his head after he came out of the room.

"It's not good, Martha," he said to the woman, who was hanging on to Lem for dear life. "I won't lie to you. I thought for sure I had everything sewn up and cleaned out good, but this . . . this isn't the way it's supposed to be. I'm real sorry."

Slocum was convinced that bringing him back in the saddle hadn't done him any good either, but Doc Witherspoon said, "Don't go laying blame, son. You got him back here as quick as you could, and with that shot-up wing 'a yours, too. That's the important part. Some things," he added with a sigh, "just aren't meant to be."

Slocum didn't feel much better about it, though.

That evening, there wasn't much of any ruckus during the hands' dinner, and not during theirs. Doc had said that Jack might live another day or two, but that was it, and they were all grieving in advance.

Over coffee, Lem said, "Slocum, Martha and me talked it over, and we'd like to bury Jack back in our family plot, if you ain't got no objections. He'll be with good folk."

Slocum nodded his head. "I can't think of better, Lem. I think Jack'd be proud."

Lem pulled a slip of paper from his pocket. "Martha got all his information the other day. You know, where he's from, his folks' names and such, and his birthday." He smiled a little. "Said as how he laughed and asked her, was she gettin' this stuff for his tombstone." And then Lem bent his head and stopped talking.

Slocum saw a tear drizzle down his cheek, and busied himself rolling a quirlie, then lighting it.

He had almost finished the smoke when a red-eyed Martha came down the hall and joined them. Standing behind Lem's chair, her hands on his shoulders, she quietly said, "He's gone."

22

The next morning, Slocum rose with the dawn after a fitful night. He'd tossed and turned, trying to direct his dreams toward happier times, but it all came back to one thing: Jack was dead. Lem had said he'd have the local sheriff wire the boy's family, and that he'd tell them about Jack's account at the Phoenix bank. That was the only thing Slocum felt halfway decent about—at least Jack had accumulated a large sum of money to leave to his folks.

He supposed it would help.

But it still wasn't enough. He'd bet that Jack's family would a lot rather have Jack back. The damn fool kid. Wouldn't give up, no matter what. Slocum had half expected that Jack would have changed his mind—again—once they made it down to Phoenix, and tried going out on his own. He was bound to end up dead.

Slocum just didn't expect it on his watch.

Slowly, he got up, then climbed down the steps to the

main floor of the barn. Lem and Martha had offered him a room for the night, but he'd said no.

He checked Rocky and found him in fine fettle. One of Lem's boys had taken the stud back to McMurtry's place a few days ago, and pronounced him in high spirits. Actually, the hand had come home nursing a bruised leg, where the stallion had kicked him.

Never trust a quarter bred stud, Slocum reminded himself. "Only Appys, huh, Rocky?" The stallion whickered low, then nudged at Slocum's hand, testing him to see if he had a treat. Slocum gave him a lemon drop and patted his neck. "I gotta go see if Lem's up and around yet," he said to the horse, and then exited the barn.

The sun was almost up, he saw when he was out in the yard. No hands, no signs of life from the house. Deciding he must be the first one up, he pulled up a chair on the front porch and rolled himself a quirlie. Watching the sunrise, he smoked. He was about to roll a second one when he heard footsteps in the house at his back, and then someone opening the door.

It was Martha. Still red-eyed, she looked like she'd had a bad night, too. It was strange, the way both she and Lem had taken to Jack. Of course, Slocum had taken to him right off the bat, too. It was just working with him that he wasn't very fond of.

But he'd earned a place in their hearts—that was for sure. Last night, Lem had taken him out back to help him pick a burial place. When Slocum said it made no difference to him, Lem picked one. It was an unlikely place, to Slocum's mind: right next to Lem and Martha's boys, the ones who had died at the hands of Apache. The boys had been only eleven and nine when their lives were cut short.

"Morning," Martha said, not too enthusiastically.

Slocum didn't blame her. He stood up and tipped his hat, and said, "Mornin' back atcha."

"Why don't you come on in?" she said, opening the door.

"Be pleased to," he replied, stepping inside. "Still too early for the hands to be up and about?"

She nodded. "Just a tad. Lem's sleepin' late, though. He was up 'til after midnight, pacin'. Just pacin' and mutterin' to himself." She followed him to the kitchen, where she already had a pot of coffee on the stove. "Sit at the table. Go ahead. I'll get you some coffee and biscuits."

"Martha, you don't have to go waitin' on me—" Slocum began, but she cut him off.

"Hush up. I gotta do *somethin'*, and you're the only one around to do it for right now." She flipped a couple of flapjacks frying in a pan, then got Slocum his coffee and biscuits.

Later that day, he helped Lem and one of the hands dig Jack's grave. They worked in grim silence with Martha nearby, her hands folded as she silently prayed over each of the graves. Doc Witherspoon showed up at about the time they were finished with the digging, and shared his condolences with the family.

He also stayed around for the burying. A couple of Lem's boys had put together a coffin, which Martha lined with an Indian blanket—Navajo, Slocum assumed—before they gently laid Jack inside and nailed the lid shut.

The funeral was brief. Nobody knew much about him, and Slocum had only their shared adventures to relate. He limited it to the ones where Jack had actually contributed something, or done something brave, which kept his speech to a minimum. Afterward, Slocum and Lem filled in the grave while Martha continued her prayers, and when they

were finished, Doc Witherspoon left. He took a last look at
Slocum's arm, pronounced that he was healing up fine, and
went on his way.

The rest of the day went on as normal, all things considered. Most of the hands were out on the range, Martha
cooked, Lem puttered around, and Slocum? Well, he just
sat and smoked.

He thought he should go into town tomorrow and report
Jack's death to the sheriff. Get some ready-made smokes,
too, if they had any. He could only smoke so many of his own
quirlies before they began to pale. And then, he was almost
out of lemon drops for Rocky. Had to get those, too. He'd
got so that every time he entered or exited the barn, Rocky
was right there, expecting a treat. And Slocum gave him one,
sometimes two. All right, sometimes he gave him three.

He checked the time. Two o'clock. He guessed he still
had time to get there and back today. He stood up from his
porch chair and almost knocked Lem over. He hadn't even
known he was there.

"Easy, big feller," Lem said with a chuckle.

Slocum grinned at him. "How do I get from here to
town, Lem?"

"You wantin' t'go today?"

Slocum nodded.

"Well, the fastest way is for me to lead you there. You'll
get lost in these woods, sure as shootin', if I leave you to
your own self." Lem stepped down off the porch, then turned
back to Slocum. "Well, let's get goin'. I wanna be back for
supper." Then he looked past Slocum to the open door, and
shouted, "Mother, me an' Slocum are goin' into town. We'll
be back for supper!"

"Get some sugar," she called back. "Ten pounds!"

The men set off for the barn and their horses.

* * *

'Town" turned out to be something of a letdown.

It was small, for one thing. There were only four buildings: a bar/hotel/restaurant; the sheriff's office, which doubled as a town hall and the mayor's office; a general store/hardware store; and a small livery/feed store. It occurred to Slocum that Troubadour was vastly, well, overnamed, if there was such a word.

"Where's the doc's office?" Slocum wondered aloud.

"At his house," Lem answered. "Over there." He pointed into the hills and forest, but Slocum couldn't see a damned thing.

Slocum rode over to the general store and dismounted. With Lem tagging at his heels, he went inside and found lemon drops for Rocky, and—lo and behold—ready-mades for himself! He got a box of kitchen matches, too. He was about to run out.

Lem got Martha's sugar, and then the two set out for the sheriff's office, which was next door to the saloon. Slocum paused to order a beer, which came ice cold. He voiced his surprise to Lem, who said, "Yea, they haul ice down from the mountains till about the middle'a June. How you figger we keep our cold box cold?"

Slocum shrugged. "Didn't think about it, I guess."

Lem ordered a beer, too, and leaned back against the bar—two planks held up by sawhorses—to enjoy it. He took another long draw, then licked his lips. "Always better," he murmured. "Always better cold."

Slocum was enjoying his, too, but also lit the first ready-made and took a good long drag on it. He smiled. "Always better store-bought," he said in a sideways answer to Lem, who stared at him a second, then laughed.

"You mean the smokes, don'tcha?" he said.

Slocum joined in with a grin, and said, "Yup. You want one, or you still in love with that pipe?"

"It's love everlastin'," came Lem's reply. "'Sides, Martha'd kill me dead iff'n I switched over at this late date."

Slocum laughed. It was pretty damn near impossible to think of Martha hurting—let alone killing—anybody!

They were just about finished with their beers when the batwing doors swung in, and the sheriff entered. He nodded, then said, "Lem, Slocum. Any more trouble?"

Removing his hat and holding it over his heart, Lem said, "Only that the boy, Jack Tandy, passed on yesterday. We buried him in the family plot this mornin'."

The sheriff nodded. "Yeah, Doc Witherspoon reported it. I sent a rider over Prescott way to let the U.S. Marshal's Office know."

Slocum tipped his head. "Thanks. Obliged."

That meant that the U.S. marshal would have one more charge to place against Grimes. And that maybe, just maybe they'd have the new poster in Phoenix by the time he got back. He hoped so anyway.

He said, "Sheriff, I'd be obliged iff'n you could give me a paper saying as how I killed Grimes, and he's in you cemetery. They'll want it—"

"When you get back to Phoenix. I know." The sheriff reached into his back pocket and pulled out a folded paper. "Been waitin' for you to show up and ask for it," he said, handing it over.

"Thanks." Slocum unfolded it and gave it a quick read. The sheriff must have written it up just this morning, because it also reported Jack's demise. Finding it in order, he looked up and said, "Thanks, Sheriff. Obliged to you." He tucked it in his pocket, satisfied.

The sheriff asked, "Either one of you got any information on the boy's next of kin? I gotta inform them, y'know."

It was Lem's turn to dig into his pocket. "Here you go,"

he said, handing it over. "Martha got it from him before he . . . you know."

"Croaked," the lawman said matter-of-factly. "Hey, Ike, gimme a beer. On my tab."

The barkeep drew him one and set it on the bar. Just as quickly, the sheriff scooped it up. "Gotta take advantage of these cold ones while he got 'em, right, Lem?"

"Right." There was no expression that Slocum could read on Lem's face.

Slocum had copied down everything that Jack had told Martha, so he wasn't at a loss when the sheriff kept the paper, but he asked Lem, "You got a boy makin' him a headstone?"

"Yeah," Lem said. "But I already gave him what needs to be on it."

"All right."

They sipped in silence for a few more minutes, while the sheriff gossiped with the bartender, and then Slocum said, "We ought'a be startin' back if we're gonna make it for dinner, Lem."

Lem drained the last of his beer. "Yeah. Did I get her the sugar?"

"On the back'a your horse, Lem."

"Oh, yeah. Well, thanks, Sheriff. Be seein' you." He stalked out of the bar without further words, but Slocum tipped his hat, then followed along.

Once they were mounted and had ridden well out of town, Lem said, "I do hate that sheriff! He's a goddamn little pissant!"

"What'd he do to you, Lem? Seemed like a regular feller to me."

"He ain't got no heart. He ain't got no common decency! For instance, did he even tell you his name?"

Slocum had to think. "Nope," he said at last.

"See? That's just an example! It's Blacksmith, Dick Black-smith. Never tells nobody his name 'cause he'd druther be known as The Sheriff." He shook his head and grumbled under his breath, "The high-and-mighty sonofabitch!"

23

As it was the night before, conversation at the dinner table—the hands, as well as Slocum, Lem, and Martha—was limited. Mostly folks sat and stared at their plates—and ate what was on them. But there were no jovial hoots and hollers, no laughter about what they'd done that day.

Slocum decided it was time he moved on. Jack would have Lem and Martha to mourn him for a good long time, leaving no room for him. And besides, he needed to get back down to Phoenix. Not only to pick up the reward money and check for new posters, but to see Katie again. It had been too long, something he couldn't excuse since she was in the same territory with him. He'd gone all achy for her in the nights, and trying not to think of her was like telling a dying man not to think about life.

He excused himself from Martha and Lem early in the evening and wandered back to the graveyard. A stone had already been placed at its head, and he knelt and struck a match to read it. It was crudely carved, but legible.

Here Lies Jackson Tandy, it read, then the dates of birth and death, and then *A Good, Brave Boy Murdered by a Stinking Land Thief.*

Slocum figured that Lem had picked the words, until he got to the end, obviously added by Martha's orders: *We Wish Jack Was Our Own.*

Slocum left for Phoenix the next morning, after breakfasting with Lem and Martha, and listening to a few more of Lem's stories. And also accepting a parcel from Martha, to be opened when he stopped for lunch.

He left Jack's mare behind, with Lem, to do with as he wished, and he and Rocky set out at an easy lope. Rocky's lope was as pleasant to ride as his jog-trot, and they sure gained ground faster. Of course, Slocum thought, it helped that they weren't traveling with a mare in season. He stopped for lunch several miles south of where he and Jack had stopped, hobbled Rocky and got him set up with feed and water, then sat down with Martha's parcel.

It was the mother lode! And best of all, there weren't any glass do-bobs he'd have to take back!

Oh, she'd sent him a half loaf of bread, plus jam and fresh butter; the butt end of a pork roast, already sliced for sandwiches; some potatoes, salted and sliced so very thin, and fried up so crisp that they cracked in his mouth; and a load of strawberries, already sugared.

He couldn't eat it all, which, for Slocum, was saying something! But he tucked the leftovers back into their box, and saved them for later.

Sated, he whistled up Rocky, bribed him with a lemon drop, tacked him up again, and once more, started south toward Phoenix.

It was a nice day to make such a trip. The grass was green, the clover was blooming, the only sounds besides those that came from Rocky's footfalls and the little squeaks and complaints of saddle leather were the steady hum of bees on the clover and the occasional call of a crow or another desert bird.

It was the kind of day that made a fellow feel glad to be alive. And then he thought about Jack again, and his face fell. *Damn shame*, he thought, shaking his head. *Just a stupid damn shame.* He was still convinced that they could have found Jack a trade not only that he'd be good at, but that he'd enjoy. Oh, well. Too late.

He rode into the outskirts of Phoenix before dark, and skirted cotton fields and hay fields, plus fording canals and crossing the river, before he got into town proper. And he made straight for Katie's place.

She met him at the front door and hugged him so tight he was afraid his eyeballs would pop out, then asked after Jack. She cried when he told her what happened. Cried real tears. And so did the young, pretty, blond whore called Jasmine, who had been Jack's favorite. Slocum didn't blame them for it. They didn't know any better.

He left his things there, then led Rocky on down the street and settled him in at the livery. Once that was attended to— lemon drops and all—he hiked back up to Katie's.

The girls told him Katie was waiting upstairs—which seemed a little presumptuous, even for her—but upstairs he went, and tapped on her door.

"Come in, Slocum," she said. Even from out in the hall, he could tell she was still crying. And when he stepped inside the room, she turned her face away so that he wouldn't see the tears.

He knew they were there, though. He went to the edge of the bed and sat down, reaching across and pulling her close. "It's all right, Katie baby," he whispered, and she tucked her face against his broad chest. He began to rock her back and forth.

"It's all right," he soothed. "It's all right, Katie darlin'."

The following morning, Slocum woke up to, of all things, the sound of rain! A storm had moved in during the night, and Phoenix was getting a real pounding. In a city with no gutters, with no rainspouts, and hardly anything else to handle excess water, it was a major occurrence. For some, it was a major disaster.

Katie's place was new, and so was fairly watertight. But inside the place next door, an old adobe run by a Swedish madam named "Missus Kemble," they were ankle deep in water. Slocum threw in his back and hand along with several other men, and they managed to swamp out the place within a couple of hours, although it was going to take a lot of work to fix up, once it dried out.

It was no skin off Slocum's nose. He planned to be long gone by then. Up to Montana maybe. Or Colorado.

It didn't much matter really.

He went to the sheriff's office late that afternoon, and reported the murder of Jack Tandy, and also that of the now horse thief and murderer, Rupert Grimes. The sheriff wrote it all down, then had Slocum sign it.

"Don't know when we'll get paper on this new stuff," said the sheriff. He looked at Slocum as if he knew the big man's feet were itching like crazy, and the wanderlust was on him. "Tell you what. When it comes in, I'll just put it in your bank account, okay?"

Slocum gladly took him up on it. He also asked, "You got any new paper on anybody else?"

"Not a blessed soul, sorry to say."

"We'll hope for better luck the next time." He put his hand on the latch. "See you!"

Night was almost on them when he left the sheriff's office, and he headed back toward Miss Katie's, smoking a ready-made cigarette and just generally glad to be breathing in the clean, damp air.

That night was different than the night before. Yesterday, Katie had cried herself to sleep in Slocum's arms, and Slocum had drifted off soon thereafter. He had to admit that he didn't have the slightest notion why Katie would be so upset at Jack's death. She had hardly known him, after all. He had better reason to understand Jasmine's sorrow, as he learned later that she had just that morning learned she was pregnant. It was Jack's.

Slocum told her that he'd be happy to take her to California, to Jack's folks, but she turned him down. It seemed that she was far too embarrassed about being a hooker. Slocum told her she could go as Jack's wife, therefore justifying the baby as well, but she only told him she'd think about it. He hoped she'd think quick. He was leaving in the morning.

After a satisfying supper, as always, Katie and Slocum sat in the kitchen after the girls had left, talking.

He knew that she was still upset about Jack, but that she wouldn't mention it again. Last night had been her period of grieving, and that would be that. She didn't bring it up again either. Instead, she talked about little Jasmine.

Slocum didn't want to hear it, and told Katie so. He said that he only wanted to hear from Jasmine herself, and that she had until the morning because he was leaving. Katie immediately dropped the subject, but before she did, she said, "I was only worried about her."

"I know," Slocum replied softly. He got out a ready-made and scratched a sulphur tip into life. Puffing the smoke, he said, "Jack's got a real nice grave up there. Lem and his wife took quite a liking to him, and they asked to bury him in the family plot. Right next to their sons, too." He shook out his match and tossed it on his pillaged plate, where it continued to send up smoke in a tiny, curling wave.

"Right next to their boys?" Katie asked. It wasn't exactly a normal thing to do, and Slocum and Katie both knew it.

"Yeah. Seems they practically adopted him, or as close as they could get to it."

Katie just shook her head and muttered, "Right next to their own boys . . ."

Slocum blew out a long plume of white smoke and stared down at the table. "Yeah."

Later, they went upstairs to the familiarity of Katie's room, where Slocum made up for lost time, and Katie was right along with him. After their third go-round—or it might have been the fourth, Slocum had lost track—he got up and walked to the window. It had started to rain again, although it wasn't the gully-washer of earlier in the day. This was just a light but steady sprinkle of rain.

Lightning flashed in the far-off sky to the north, momentarily illuminating the interior of the room, and Slocum thought about Lem and Martha, and how things were up at their place.

He had just seated himself in the plush chair by the window and lit a cigarette when he became aware of a ruckus outside. He peeked out the window.

The sheriff was running down the center of the sloppy road—*their* sloppy road—shouting Slocum's name. Just before he opened the gate to run up to the house, Slocum opened Katie's window and called down, "What's got you so shook up at"—he glanced at the clock—"twelve thirty of an evening? Seems to me you ought'a be home with the family!"

The sheriff called back up, "I sure the hell should. But we got a situation over at the Purple Garter, and I reckon you're the only thing we've got that can take care of it."

Had the saloon sprung a leak, too? He asked, "Can't this wait till mornin'?"

24

Fifteen minutes later, a fully dressed Slocum was downstairs and jogging down the street alongside the sheriff.

"He's in the saloon," said the sheriff, mud splashing at his every footfall. "Already killed one deputy and two civilians. The civilians, 'cause one wouldn't move out of his way and the other one on general principle, and the deputy because he tried to arrest him for the other two murders." They stepped up onto the boardwalk, and were out of the rain. "I swear, I don't know what's happened to people. I just plain don't get it."

Slocum tried to get information that was more pertinent. "What's his name?"

"Don't know. Nobody's ever seen him before, though. Might be from outta the territory."

Slocum nodded. They were nearing the Purple Garter, and all he could think was, *Thank God Jack's not here*. If the sheriff thought the body count was high now . . .

They reached the saloon. The sheriff stayed well back

from the windows, out of sight of the killer, but said, "Good luck, Slocum. This one, you can kill. The territory'll pay."

"How much?"

"At least two thousand. One for the deputy, and one for the two civilians."

"Nice to know us civilians are worth so much . . ." Slocum muttered as he put a hand on the batwing doors and pushed his way into the saloon.

The sheriff hadn't known the gunman, but Slocum recognized him right away. He was Rance Fortney, wanted for multiple murders all over the West—five in California alone—the last time he'd seen any paper on him. And that had been a while back.

Don't get cocky, he told himself as he walked up to the bar. *He's dangerous.*

Fortney must have told the other patrons to act normally, because they were spread out, some at the bar, some at tables, and their conversation was kept low. No hoots and hollers from this crowd. But if he'd been playing poker with them, he would have made a mint. Every single one of them was showing a "tell," which let him know that they were plenty nervous. Fortney was at a table in the far corner of the room, his back to the wall.

Slocum turned to the bartender and ordered a beer. Fortunately, it was a different man than the one who'd been in charge the day he and Jack took Silas Recker out of there and off to jail.

No bodies were in evidence. He supposed Fortney'd had them dragged out back, or at least out of sight. Smart.

The barkeep brought his beer, and he took a few sips before he turned his back to the bar and leaned against it casually. He was careful to hold his beer with his left hand, leaving his right hand to hang free. Its elbow was cocked on the bar top, ready to slide the hand down to his Colt at a moment's notice.

As he stood there, slowly sipping his beer, he remembered that he hadn't asked the sheriff his name. He kept meaning to, but something always threw it off. If he got out of this alive, he was going to ask him, straight on.

He wished he knew what kind of firepower Fortney was carrying. He liked to know what the odds were. Not that it mattered that much this time. If the sheriff had told him it was Fortney, he would've gone back to sleep. It was, after all, the town's problem, not Slocum's. But he was stuck with it now.

On the other hand, Fortney must be worth a heap of money, all told . . .

He checked his situation. Fortney wasn't a straight shot from here. He was at a rear table, so that precluded just shooting him. There were too many men sitting between them.

He checked the tables, and found he was in luck—there was a table against the wall at the side of the room that nobody had chosen to sit at. From there, he'd have a clean shot. He hoped.

Carrying his beer, he slowly ambled toward the table, excusing himself when he came too close to any man's back or side as he walked. Just a drifter, in town for a drink, that was him. Not looking for trouble, no sir.

He finally reached the table he was aiming at, and pulled out a chair, his back to the window. It wasn't his favorite place—Fortney already had that one—and he hoped to hell that the man didn't have a friend outside. He'd just have to trust that the sheriff had finished clearing the street out front.

He scooted back a bit and slung his boots up on another chair, took a pull on his beer, and eased his hand down toward his Colt. The hammer was resting on a full chamber. He'd checked that before he walked in.

Fortney hadn't even looked at him, except when he walked in.

The only easy shot he could get off would be under the table, which would hit Fortney in the side. If he aimed a little higher, he had a chance of taking him through the heart, but that was a tough one. Fortney, a big, blond man built like an ox, kept moving his arm around.

But Slocum was patient. He waited until Fortney's arm was comfortably propped on the table before he drew his Colt.

The shot rattled the glass and scared most of the already frightened patrons out of their seats. Except for Fortney. He had fallen, face first, on the table.

"Sit down!" Slocum ordered, and men dropped their butts into chairs with an echoing thud.

He pushed back his chair and made his way over to Fortney's body. He hoped. Fortney had lived long enough to draw his gun, which now dangled uselessly from his forefinger. If he'd been another second slower . . .

But Fortney was dead, all right. Slocum slid the gun off the other man's finger and stuck it through his own belt, then felt the man's neck for a pulse, just in case.

Nope. Dead as a hammer.

Slocum turned toward the bartender, who had dropped the glass he was polishing, and said, "Go get the sheriff. I left him right outside."

The man didn't say a word, just scampered from behind the bar and out through the batwing doors. It wasn't five seconds before the sheriff opened them again and came striding in, his gun out and ready.

When he spotted Slocum, sitting beside Fortney's body, he walked over gingerly and asked, "Is it safe?"

Several of the townsmen answered for Slocum. Most were proud that they'd lived through it, while several were still in a state of shock.

Slocum let them—and the blood pooling on the tabletop and beginning to drip to the floor—answer for him. But he asked one question. "Sheriff, what the hell's your name?"

The sheriff looked surprised, but said, "Sorry, didn't I give it before?"

"Nope. And we been doin' a lotta business lately."

"It's Henderson. Gale Henderson."

Slocum stood up. He didn't want to get blood on his boots. He said, "Well, Gale, there he is. You'd best check with the territorial marshal to see what he's worth. I reckon it could be up around ten thousand by now, dependin' on who-all he's killed. Maybe more."

And with that, he went back to his own table, picked up his beer, and downed it. Maybe it had been a good thing he'd come out with the sheriff, after all.

He was halfway to the batwing doors when the sheriff called, "Hey, Slocum!"

He stopped and turned around. "What?"

Henderson smiled. "Come back anytime, pardner."

Slocum returned the smile. "I will, Gale," he said. "I will. And I'll see you come mornin'."

Watch for

**SLOCUM AND THE GHOST OF ADAM
WEYLAND**

387th novel in the exciting SLOCUM series
from Jove

Coming in May!